# The Adventures of

# Sue Kettle
# (Mummy Otter)

The Adventures of Sue Kettle © Copyright 2003 by Norman Bailey

Illustrations © Michelle Caines & Kevin Bolton

A catalogue record of this book is available from the British Library

First Edition: November 2003

ISBN: 1-84375-068-6

To order additional copies of this book please visit:
http://www.upso.co.uk/normanbailey

Published by: UPSO Ltd
5 Stirling Road, Castleham Business Park,
St Leonards-on-Sea, East Sussex TN38 9NW United Kingdom
Tel: 01424 853349  Fax: 0870 191 3991
Email: info@upso.co.uk   Web: http://www.upso.co.uk

# The Adventures of

## Sue Kettle
## (Mummy Otter)

*by*

# Norman Bailey

*Illustrated by*
*Michelle Caines & Kevin Bolton*

# UPSO

# CHAPTER ONE

# FRIEND OR FOE.

We are a family of water otters. There are six of us at the moment. Robbie is my mate. I am Sue and we have four pups. Their names are Tina, Kevin, Lee and the youngest is Nigel. Our family name is Kettle. We live in the New Forest in Dorset. Our family has lived here for many generations.

Life can be very dangerous at times but we also have a lot of fun. So I would like to share some of our experiences with you.

One spring morning we woke to a warmish day. My first job is to get the pups to wash and tidy themselves up. Then they will follow Robbie and myself into the river to catch some breakfast. They are still learning how to catch fish. Nigel needs quite a bit more practice because he tends to play about instead of learning. The other three are doing very well so far. I will soon be able to leave them to catch their own food. Then I will have some more time to myself.

As we live mainly on fish, we live near rivers and lakes. On this particular day Robbie leads the way to one of our usual fishing grounds and the four pups follow eagerly because like me they are hungry.

After about an hour without any luck at all Robbie decides to investigate further along the river to see why. This spot usually supplies us with a good source of food. When he comes back he tells us that some humans have nets across the river. This is what is stopping the fish from coming our way. So we all go to a lake further into the forest and fish for our breakfast there. When we have filled our bellies we decide to go back to the river near our home to rest in the sun for a while.

Suddenly our peace is shattered by a loud bang. All of us started to run to the river for safety. When I looked back Nigel was limping along instead of running after us. He was dragging one of his back legs. I noticed that it was bleeding. Robbie ran back and helped him into the river. Then they followed us out of sight to safety.

When I took a close look at Nigel's wound I could see that he had been shot. Fortunately it was only a flesh wound. So it should heal up quite quickly. Poor Nigel. He had to rest for a few days so we took fish back to him for his dinner.

We assumed that the humans shot at us because we eat fish and they wanted our share as well. Or perhaps they just shot at us for "fun". We stayed away from that part of the river for several days just in case they decided to shoot at us again.

The lake that supplied us with our food during these few days seemed to be a bit short of fish. So we had to go back to our usual spot in the river. Perhaps the humans had gone away by now. But if they were on holiday they could still be nearby.

When we swam around the bend in the river we noticed to our dismay that there were some young humans playing on the bank. One of them was very young and not at all steady on her feet. When they saw us they decided to try to frighten us away. They threw sticks and stones into the river to try and hit us. Fortunately they threw very badly and missed us. Also we can swim very fast. Even Nigel is getting back to his proper speed now that his leg is healing up. We were very pleased that it was only the children here today and not the adults with that gun again.

Suddenly the very young one slipped as she threw a big stick at us. She toppled and fell into the river. There was a loud splash as she hit the water. This frightened our pups even more. So they swam away even faster around the bend and home to safety.

The little girl in the river was shouting and screaming. She was very frightened. Her friends tried to reach her but could not. Also the river was to deep for them to step into. So I called to Robbie to give me a hand to help the little girl or she would surely drown. I swam underneath her to keep her as near to the surface as possible and Robbie grabbed hold of her blouse with his teeth and tried to swim to the riverbank.

Tim, Kevin and Lee had swum back to see where we were and what we were trying to do. As usual Nigel was nowhere to be seen. "What could he be up to"? I said. "Probably scared," said Robbie. "He will still be in our home!"

We swam as fast as we could and managed to reach

*We swam as fast as we could and managed to reach the riverbank but it was too high for us to climb up and pull the little girl onto the safety of the riverbank.*

the riverbank but it was too high for us to climb up and pull the little girl onto the safety of the riverbank. The other children had all run off in fright.

Little did we know that Nigel saw what we were doing and had gone to try to get some help. He did a very dangerous thing. He ran to the camp where the humans were staying. He stopped at the camps edge to quickly check what was going on there. Was it safe he thought? How could he attract the attention and get them to follow him. He noticed that one of the humans had put their mobile phone on the ground by their foot. Because he knew just how serious the situation was he decided to chance it. He ran as fast as he could and snatched the phone with his teeth and started to run back towards the river. The humans saw him and gave chase. Fortunately they cannot run as fast as Nigel even with his bad leg. It's a good job it was healing up so well. His heart was beating so fast and loud that he was sure everyone could hear it. He was scared but also very excited.

By the time he reached the riverbank his leg hurt so much that he could not run any further. He collapsed on the ground and lay there exhausted and hurting.

"There he is", they shouted! "Get him and the phone quickly". Just as they reached him, the children ran out of the forest shouting "she is in the river, quickly help her."

The adults stopped in their tracks and looked into the river. Then they spotted the five otters and their little girl struggling to stay near the bank. Two of the humans rushed to where they were, leaned over and grabbed the little girl and pulled her onto the safety of dry land. We all swam away just in case they thought we were trying to hurt her. Nigel had recovered enough to dive into the river and join us as we swam to safety.

We had to feed the next morning as we do every day, so Robbie went out first to make sure that it was safe for us to follow and fish for our breakfast. He came back a few minutes later and said that there were two adults there but he couldn't see any guns. So we decided to take a chance because we were very hungry. Robbie and myself went first and our children followed us at a bit of a distance for safety.

As the two adults saw us approaching they called out and the little girl that was in the river yesterday appeared and walked down to them. They had several buckets with them as they walked slowly down to the rivers edge. They were looking at Robbie and seemed to be talking to him in very soft and gentle voices as though not to frighten him. Then they put the buckets down and one of them pulled a big fish out and put it on the ground. It was jumping around all over the place. Then the two of them stepped back, turned around and walked very slowly away.

The little girl stayed where she was. Only she sat down near the jumping fish. She was laughing as she tried to catch it. But of course it was too slippery for her. Robbie got out of the water and slowly walked towards the little girl. He peeped into the buckets and started to call to us. "The buckets are full", he shouted. So we all ran up the bank towards the buckets. We have not had lunch served to us before so this was a rare treat. "Yippee", they all shouted as they got stuck into breakfast. Of course Nigel had to knock one of the buckets over and the fish jumped all over the place.

# The Adventures of Sue Kettle

We certainly had a good meal that day. The adults stopped about thirty feet away to watch us. The little girl stroked the pups and could not stop giggling. Then the adults called to her to go with them. I think that she wanted to stay with us for a while but when they called to her again she got up and slowly walked away towards the adults. Then they all walked back to the campsite.

We never saw them again which was such a pity. The buckets were not there the next day either. So we assume that they had gone home. Perhaps the fish were a thank you for helping the little girl. We like to think so. Also perhaps they will come back to see us one day. We do hope so. So now everything is back to normal. Nigel's leg is fully recovered thank goodness. Also we seem to have lots of fish in our rivers again.

Well that's all for now. I hope that you enjoyed my little story about my family and how we live.

Sue Kettle.

Mummy Otter.

"LIKE A FISH OUT OF WATER!"

# CHAPTER TWO

# A LESSON TO BE LEARNT

Hello again! I hope that you enjoyed my first story about our life here in the New Forest. This is another story that I remember well. We all should learn from our mistakes. Especially our young ones. I hope that this story is one that you can learn from. Only time will tell.

This summer has been the hottest that I can remember. Being so hot has a dramatic effect on our way of life because the rivers and lakes are drying up. I do hope that it rains soon.

We are travelling further than ever before to get our food. This takes up a lot of time and makes the children very tired. But at least we did find a big lake that seemed to have plenty of fish in but it was on the edge of a holiday site for humans. There are more here than usual because of the lovely weather. Lots of them come here to fish in the lake. So we have got competition. If they saw us in the lake they threw stones at us to frighten us away. But we did not go too far because we need the fish to live. They seem to want all the fish to themselves. Why can't they share?

One day we did not have a lot of luck with our fishing because they kept throwing things at us. This made it dangerous for us. I was getting very worried in case my children got hurt. By the end of the day the children were still hungry but we decided that it was too dangerous for us to stay here any longer. I gathered the children together but where was Nigel? As usual he was nowhere to be found. Suddenly he came running around the lake with a big fish in his mouth. A few yards behind him came two men running as fast as they could. Fortunately we Otters can run very fast so they had very little chance of catching him. He spotted me and as we all started running home he followed as fast as his little legs would carry him. When we had left the men a long way behind we stopped and shared the fish between us.

I asked Nigel how he got the fish. He told me that he saw the two men catch several large fish and then they started to pack up their things to go. So he followed them, being careful not to be seen. They were staying in a tent on the edge of the human site. So when they put the fish down to put the things away in the tent he rushed towards the fish and grabbed one. Of course he then ran off as fast as he could. They soon spotted him and gave chase. But as you already know they did not catch him.

I told him off because what he did was very dangerous. He could have been caught or worse still he could have been shot. But I do not think he took much notice, as he was too busy eating his ill-gotten gains. I must admit that the fish was lovely and we had all eaten plenty now.

A couple of days later to our surprise we noticed a stranger in our lake. We do not normally like strange Otters in our area as we see them as a threat to our fish stock. We do share but only in our family. Robbie chased him away immediately. Fortunately he was quite young so he was no match for him. I kept my eyes on my young and also all around just in case he came with more of his family. Then we really would be in trouble.

What the new Otter did was to run away but then come back and watched us from a hiding place that he had found.

As usual Nigel was up to his tricks again. He decided that it was easier to follow the fishermen back to their tents and steal their fish than to catch his own. This is very true, but humans can be clever sometimes as well. But this time he managed once again to get some extra fish for us. But I told him not to do it again as he would easily get caught. So he promised me that he would not.

The strange Otter had been watching all of this from his hiding place. And decided to give Nigels idea a try. What a good idea he thought. How easy this looks. So the next day he crept around the lake and hid. We did not see him until the fishermen picked up their fish and headed back to the campsite. We saw the strange Otter following them.

A few minutes later just as we were all about go home we heard him shout and squeal. Robbie went to investigate. What he saw was a home-made trappers cage outside a tent. Inside the cage going frantic was the Otter. The humans had caught him. What could we do to help him? "We cannot just leave him there," said Nigel, "they may kill him."

When it got dark Robbie crept into the campsite to have a look to see if there was any way to get him out of the cage. It was just a basic home-made cage thank goodness. The door just had a rope attached to the top. The humans had waited until the Otter went into the cage where they had placed the fish and let the door drop shut. Nigel suddenly realised that my advice to him was correct.

We all got together and discussed a way to open the door. Somehow we had to get hold of the rope and lift it. But we were not tall enough. Then Robbie told us of his plan. The trap was at the bottom of the trees by the tent so we would have to be extra quiet or the humans would hear us.

Robbie told us how his plan should work. "It would be very dangerous" said Lee, my youngest. But she knew that we had to give it a try.

I took Lee and Kevin to the edge of the site for safety. Even though they wanted to stay and help. Then the three of us hid but made sure that we could see what was going on.

Robbie took the rope that was attached to the door and climbed a little way up the tree and out onto a branch. Nigel climbed a branch underneath Robbie's and waited until he dropped the rope over the top branch and almost down to him. Tim waited by the cage and told the trapped Otter to wait for his signal.

Nigel grabbed hold of the rope in his mouth and jumped off of the branch. Making sure that he did not let go because if the humans heard them they would all be in a lot of trouble. He hit the ground in seconds. Fortunately the cage door was now open but only for a few moments. As soon as Nigel jumped, Tim told the trapped Otter to run towards the cage door. He reached the door just as it opened and ran straight out. He followed Tim and the other two as they ran for safety.

The humans soon came out of the tent to see what all the noise was about. But they were far too slow and so we all escaped to our home. The new Otter came with us of course. Where else could he go?

We gave him a chance to explain why he was here by himself. He said that his family had been attacked and he ran away. He did not know if they were dead or alive. He asked if he could stay with us. We said yes of course as long as he obeyed our rules. He was very happy with this. We called him Tricky, as this seemed to suit him.

He stayed with us for quite some time until one day he told us that he wanted to move to another part of the forest. Also that our Lee wanted to go with him. He seemed to think that they could be happy together. I think so to. They can both fish properly nowadays and they seemed to know all the other things that they need to know to be safe and happy. So we wished them well and off they went. We see them sometimes when we go to fish in their area or when they come to ours.

The weather was getting back to normal now and we are getting thunderstorms and lots of rain. Thank goodness. So the rivers and lakes are filling up nicely.

# Norman Bailey

I hope that you enjoyed this little story and perhaps have learnt something from it.
Bye for now

Sue Kettle

Mummy Otter.

# CHAPTER THREE

# THE SWAMP AND THE LOST CHILDREN

Hello again. I hope you enjoyed my two other stories. (That is of course if you have read them.) Today I would like to tell you about another very worrying but also exciting day that I remember.

It was early summer and the weather was quite pleasant. The lakes and rivers were about normal level. Also the fish were plentiful. So we had plenty to eat.

We had just finished eating our dinner (fish of course. It's our favourite food.) We were trying to keep out of the way of the fishermen that come here quite a bit at this time of year. We usually head for the island in the middle because the fishermen usually fish from around the outside of the lake. But a few do row over to the island. It is much easier for us because we can swim across. One part of the lake is only about three feet deep. But the mud is very deep there. If they try to wade across at this point they are likely to get bogged down in the mud.

We laid on the island in the sunshine to have a rest and to let our dinner go down. Also our young ones can have a play. It is Robbies turn to keep them amused today. All the same they still try to get me to join in. usually I pretend to be asleep. But this does not always work. But today I managed to fall off to sleep.

I woke to the sound of people talking. They were coming our way. It was a man with two children. They were about seven or eight years old. The man was rowing a small boat. The children shouted because they had seen our children and Robbie playing on the bank. The boat was heading for the same part of the island so I called out to everyone that we must hide. We dived into the water and swam to the other side of the island. We felt safer there.

We could hear the children giggling as they tried to get out of the little boat. Robbie crept through the reeds to see just what the people were doing. We waited amongst the reeds just in case they decided to come our way. Then we only had to leap into the water and swim to safety.

It was getting a bit late. Almost time for us to head back home for the night. Suddenly Robbie shouted to me that he thought that the children were in trouble. When the man stepped out of the boat he accidentally pushed it out into the lake. Just too far for him to reach. The children tried to use the oars to get back to the man but they were not having any luck. The more they tried, the further the boat went out into the lake. Then one of the children lost one of the oars and as the other child tried to get it with his oar he also lost an oar. So now both oars were floating in the lake were no one could reach them. The man was getting very worried by now so he decided to try and wade out to the boat. That was a very big mistake because as I said earlier the lake may only be three feet deep but the mud is even deeper. Before he had gone very far the mud was almost up to his knees. So the water was up to his chest. If he struggled at all the water would soon be over his head and he would drown.

Robbie called to Nigel to follow him and they swam towards the boat. The idea was for them to push the boat to safety. But as soon as the two children saw them swimming towards them they got frightened and started to move to one side of the boat. So they swam away before the boat was tipped over. If the boat had gone over we were sure that the children would drown. It is all right for us because we are very good swimmers but we were not even sure that the children can swim even a little. Also there are a lot of weeds and reeds all over the lake floor. These tend to wrap around people's legs and pull them under the water.

There was a little bit of wind that was blowing the boat towards the lakes edge. So we decided to get Nigel to follow but not to close. But near enough to keep an eye on them. We decided that the man was in most danger so we would try to help him if we could. He seemed to have the sense not to struggle but he was still waist high and in quite a bit of danger. Robbie told me to follow him into the reeds where we were hiding earlier. So off we went leaving our children to keep watch over the man. In the reeds we found a lump of timber that Robbie had spotted earlier. We needed to get it into the water and float it to the man. Then perhaps he could pull himself out of the mud by using the log as a lever. It was worth a try. There was not much else we could do. We pushed and we pulled and we pulled and pushed. We bit through weeds and reeds to make way for the log. Eventually we got the log into the water. It was a very hard task for us because it was very heavy and we are not very big. But we had to do it.

As we were pushing the log through the water towards the man I looked towards the far bank. To my horror I noticed that the boat was already on the edge of the lake. That would not have been too bad but the boat seemed to be empty. Also I could not see my Nigel anywhere. I pushed the log even faster now because I wanted to go and find out what had happened.

I knew Robbie had noticed as well because he was also in top gear now. When we approached the man he did not seem frightened of us. In fact he seemed to know that we wanted to help him. I must admit that he also looked very surprised at what we were doing.

Robbie stayed with the others to make sure that the man was all right while I swam to the far bank to see if I could find out where my Nigel and the two children were. I was in such a hurry that I did not see the ducks feeding in the reeds and they had not seen me. When I suddenly appeared in front of them they flew into the air in fright.

When I looked back to the island I could see that the man was now on the log and paddling towards me. Robbie and our children were following him. I hurried onto the bank and started to look for Nigel and the children. I could not see them but I knew that Nigel knew his way around this area so I knew that he would not get lost.

There are several paths leading from the lake so I just had to find out which one they had taken. I checked several pathways before I spotted some young branches that had been broken off. When I had a closer look I could see that they had been bitten through. Wonderful I thought. Nigel was leaving me a trail to follow.

The path that he was taking was not leading to safety but was leading further into the forest. I guessed that he was following the children because if he had been by himself he would have just gone home and waited for us there. He is such a caring young Otter. Just like his father.

I followed his trail but also just in case Robbie followed, I made the trail bigger by biting off even more branches. Now they had an easy trail to follow. The ferns and trees got taller and thicker the further we went into the forest. But I knew that I still had to follow so that I could find my boy and hopefully the two children.

Quite a while later (and a lot of branch chewing) I came across a clearing with a stream running by it. I could see the two children sitting by the stream. I think they were frightened because they were crying.

Nigel saw me before I saw him because he had been watching the children while hiding amongst the ferns. He had heard the children say that they were cold tired and hungry. But he decided to stay in hiding because he did not want to frighten them. It is cold and damp with all the tall trees around. It is ok for us Otters because we have a lovely warm coat that even keeps us warm in the cold water. But the children only had tee shirts and shorts on.

*His foot was bleeding so the children picked him up and took him to the stream to bathe it.*

I told Nigel to stay near the children but to keep out of sight and wait for me to get back with some help. Then I raced back along the track to find the others. I just hope that they were following the trail that we had left.

It was not long before I met Robbie and my other children coming towards me. "Hoorah" I said. Then I noticed that the man was following them. Even better I thought. Somehow he had guessed what was happening. What they had done was to jump up and down and round and round excitedly and then ran towards the path that we had marked out for them. Humans are very slow compared to us but at least he was coming the right way.

When Robbie saw me he got very excited because he knew that he had done the right thing by following the trail. Not long after I met Robbie we came near to the ferns where I left Nigel to keep an eye on the children. But Nigel was not amongst the reeds. There he was cuddled up between the two children. They were bathing his paw in the stream. Their dad walked up to them and gave them a big hug and then he knelt down and had a look at Nigel's paw. Nigel said that he had been hiding amongst the ferns when he put his foot on some glass and cut himself. He had screamed out and the children saw him. His foot was bleeding so the children picked him up and took him to the stream to bathe it. They were not frightened of him at all.

The man carried Nigel all the way back to the lake. Then he layed him down on the grass and had another look at his paw. He said that it would be ok if Nigel did not walk on it too much. The children both gave Nigel a hug and then they all thanked us very much for all of our help. Then they turned around and walked away.

We helped Nigel get back to our home and there he rested for a while. We even got his fish for him for a couple of days until his paw was better. He deserved it didn't he. Robbie thanked the children for all that they had done and told them how grown up they had been.

That's all for today. I hope that you have enjoyed this little story. Just remember that if you can help someone without putting yourself in danger, please do so. It does make you feel so good inside.
Bye for now.

Sue Kettle.

Mummy Otter.

"TESTING THE WATER"

# CHAPTER FOUR

# A FRIEND IN NEED

Hello again children. I hope you are fit, well and happy today. I am still here in The New Forest with Robbie and our children.

Today I would like to tell you a story about a herd of animals that did not want to make friends with anyone. Well not at first anyway.

A couple of years ago in late spring, Robbie and I were resting on the bank of the big lake after lunch one day. The children were quite young at the time and as usual were causing havoc among the birds on and around the big lake.

They were just learning how to catch their own food. Which of course makes life so much easier for Robbie and myself. Their swimming had improved such a lot recently, thanks to Robbie taking lots of time to teach them. Now they could dive in very quietly and sneak up on their dinner. But they seemed to use this for sneaking up on the ducks, geese, swans and any other birds feeding on the lake. They would swim underneath them and suddenly surface right in front of them. The birds were always chasing them away. But it was all in good fun.

On this day we saw a herd of about thirty cows coming through the forest towards us where we were resting. They did not seem in much of a rush so we ignored them at first. A lot of creatures come this way for a drink and a rest.

It was only when they were about fifteen metres away from us that they started to charge. Once they cleared the bracken they came even faster towards us.

All the birds on the bank either ran or flew onto the lake. They knew that the cows could not get to them there.

Also the animals ran as fast as they could to get out of the way. The cows are much bigger and heavier than any of us. I called my youngsters to follow me and dived into the lake with them close behind. Robbie was close behind them making sure that they followed me to safety.

The cows were different from any that we have ever seen before. Their bodies looked the same but they had huge horns. Much bigger than any we had seen before. The sight of these huge horns was enough to frighten most of the creatures in the forest.

The cows stopped at the edge of the lake and started to drink some water. When they had finished drinking, one of them spoke to us. Or should I say "bellowed" at us. She said "we are much bigger and stronger than any of you and could kill any of you with a flick of our horns. So keep out of our way. If we come here to drink you must all leave at once? If we go to a field to graze you must stay away until we leave. Do you all understand?"

No one answered her so she said it again. Only this time much more ferociously. We answered by making our way to the other side of the lake and going home. We all hoped that they were just passing through. But somehow we did not think so.

The next time we wanted to eat we made our way to the big lake as usual. There were always plenty of fish there for us to eat. The local river was ok but there were not nearly as many fish there. So it made sense for us to fish in the big lake.

When we got to the edge of the trees near the bank of the lake we spotted the long horn cows drinking there again. When one of them spotted us coming towards them they shouted at us and told us to go away and stay away or we would be in trouble.

As we had our four children with us we decided to go to the river to catch our dinner today. We could only hope that the cows move to another part of the forest soon.

At the river we came across a lot of our friends that usually meet us by the big lake at meal times. All of them had been warned not to go to the big lake again while the cows were about. Even Bertie Boar and his family decided that there were too many cows for them to stand up to. So what chance had the rest of us got?

We all ate and drank and then rested by the river. Whilst we rested we chatted about a way to make the cows share the big lake with us all. As it did not actually belong to anyone group of creatures. We have always shared with everyone. Unfortunately not one of us came up with a solution that day. But we all promised to keep trying. Also we assumed that we would be eating by the river for a while now.

The next day when we all met, Bertie boar came over to us and said that the new forest ponies that lived nearby had also had a lot of problems with the cows the previous day. As they were grazing in a field next to the main motorway through the forest, they noticed a couple of young cows (calves) walking along the road. Of course the ponies knew just how dangerous this was as lots of cars come along day and night. Some of them driving very fast. So they decided to try and help them back through one of the gates to safety. They jumped the fence and landed near the cows and tried to get them to follow to a gate just down the road. Of course the cows were very young and did not understand the danger they were in.

"Go away you nasty ponies or I will tell our mum and you will be in lots of trouble," one of them said. But the ponies still decided to get them to safety. They knew it was the best thing to do. We have always tried to help each other here in the forest. Eventually the ponies surrounded the cows and forced them through a gate into the field. They saw the herd of cows not far away and decided to take the two young ones back to them.

As they approached the herd the two young cows started running towards them. But they started shouting that the ponies were bullying them and had threatened to hurt them. This made all the cows stop, look up and then charge at the ponies. One of them tried to explain that they had only helped them. But that was a waste to time and he nearly got gored for his trouble. They managed to escape by jumping over a couple of fences and running as fast as they could to safety.

For the next few weeks we all kept well away from the cows. We all agreed that it would be safer that way. But they still would not leave us alone. They chased the deer if they got too close to the herd. Also they frightened a lot of the birds on the big lake. They had to fly onto the water and then they could only use the island in the middle to rest. At least the cows could not get to them there.

One morning when we were in the river fishing we saw one of the young cows coming our way. He was heading towards a group of ponies grazing on the river edge. She shouted to them and said "move out of the way I want to drink here. Go now or I will call my mum. She will make you all move. Hurry up and move. Now".

Because they did not move straight away she decided to charge at them. Just as she got close, they parted and she stumbled through the middle of them and straight into the river. Unfortunately there was a lot of mud in this stretch and the silly cow got stuck up to her middle. The more she struggled the more stuck she became. Eventually she knew she could not get out and decided to stay still. Very sensible we thought. Now all she wanted was for us to help her. The ponies said why should they help. She had been nothing but trouble to them. Robbie and I managed to convince them that she needs our help even though she has been very nasty. If we left her there she could die. Now the problem was how to get her out! We knew that the Forest Rangers had some rope on the porch of their cabin. That would be very useful we thought.

Robbie spotted a family of crows nearby. So he ran over to them and asked if they could help us. They said that they would fly to the Forest Rangers hut and get the rope. They could manage it if they pulled it out straight and carried it between them. So off flew ten crows at full speed.

It was not long before they came back with the rope. The senior crow was called Charlie and he said that the Rangers had spotted them just as they flew off with the rope. They had run to their range rover and were following them.

Robbie took one end of the rope in his mouth and dived into the river. He swam under the young cow and then jumped onto her back. He did this twice so that the rope was nice and secure just behind her front legs. Then he took the end back to the riverbank.

The ponies let him loop the two ends around their necks and then they grabbed them in their mouths.

I told them that on the count of three they were to start pulling the rope by walking away from the river. On the count of three they started pulling with all their might. Slowly the stuck cow started to move. Just a little to start with and then a bit more until suddenly she popped out of the mud and with a little more pulling she was on the river bank safe and sound. Just at this moment the Forest Rangers appeared. They looked absolutely amazed at what was going on.

They got out of the range rover and walked over to the ponies. Then they untied the rope from around their necks. The two ponies then trotted a few yards away. Then the Rangers took hold of the rope and walked towards the cow. Very slowly so as not to frighten her any more. The poor thing was covered in mud from the river.

One of the rangers held onto the rope while the other one fetched a bucket and filled it with water from the river. They then washed all the mud from the cow. She was so stunned and frightened that she just stood still while all this was going on. They checked to make sure she was all right and then let her go. A quick slap on her rump and she was running across the field towards where her mother was feeding with the other cows. She needed to be near her mother so that she would feel safe again. This had been a very frightening experience for her.

The Rangers went to gather the rope that we had used but my four youngsters decided to play a game and ran off with it. They followed them all the way across the field and only got the rope back when my four tried to go through a fence and got it all tangled.

The Rangers laughed as they untangled the rope and put it in their vehicle. Then they drove off knowing that everything was all right now. They had got used to strange things happening here in the forest.

We thanked the ponies and the crows for all their help. Then we all finished off our hunt for food before we set off for home again.

Some time later as I was getting my youngsters ready for bed, along came Olive and Oscar Owls. They hooted to us that the cows would like to meet us all by the big lake the next morning at breakfast time. This was certainly a surprise to all of us. What can they want now?

The next day after I had got our four to wash and get ready to go out, Robbie and I told them that he would go to the big lake with me but they were to stay hidden in the bracken just in case there was any trouble.

When we got there we found that a lot of other forest creatures were already there. The senior cow was already talking to them. Quietly and softly and not angrily like before. When she saw us arrive she stopped talking to the others and looked towards us. Her words were very sincere. "Those two there saved my child" she said. Very firm but with a lot of meaning. "I know some of you others helped but it was them that organized everyone. I know us cows have been awful to you all since we arrived here. We do that so we can get what we want. We have not been anywhere where the animals stick together and help each other. You even helped us when we did not deserve your help. We would all like to thank every one of you very much for all you have done for us.

Tomorrow we will be moving on to another part of the forest. But we would like to stop here sometimes when we are in the area. That is of course if you do not mind."

She was looking straight at me when she said this. So I said very loudly, "does anyone mind if they stop here sometimes." "Of course no one would mind." Shouted Bertie Boar.

Now every one was happy and we got on with our lives again.

The next day they moved away as they said they would. Since then they have been back a few times for some food and water. But they have always been friendly to us all. Even the young cows are polite and friendly to us now. How they have grown since our first meeting. My four have grown up and moved away but I have four more to look after now. I try to teach my young not to be selfish and to always help others if they can. Those cows have learnt haven't they?

That's all for now children until the next story. Just remember to help others if you can. Maybe someday you will need help yourself just like that cow.
Bye for now.

Sue Kettle.

Mummy Otter.

# CHAPTER FIVE

# GUNS DANGER AND LOVE

Hello again children. Welcome to my fifth story. I hope you enjoy it.

It is all about guns danger and love. So out of despair can come some happiness if you are lucky.

I remember a few years ago just after we had finished eating our dinner and were relaxing on the bank of the big lake in the sunshine, I was thinking how my children were growing up too fast, but of course I knew that I must let them go some day soon. Our home would soon be too small for us all.

All of a sudden I heard a loud splash a few yards away on the lake. What could that be I thought? Robbie swam over to where the splash seemed to be in the water. Immediately he called "danger" so we all dived into the lake and swam to what we hoped would be a safe distance away.

Robbie called us all together and said that a pigeon falling into the lake caused the splash. It had been shot and was dead. We had not heard a loud bang, so we believe that an air rifle was used. We guessed that the person or people were still hiding because we had not heard or seen any humans around.

We know just how dangerous guns can be so we headed back home straight away. Better to be safe than sorry as my dad always told me.

All the birds on the lake had flown away to escape from the danger. Only Ratty Rat and his family stayed. But at least they had their rat holes to hide in.

Luckily we had just eaten so we did not need to go out until the next morning. We got up early and just to be on the safe side decided to feed in the little lake today.

When we got there we were very distressed to see several rabbits and three rats laying dead on the bank. Whoever was killing them was doing it for so called fun. Not for food.

Robbie kept watch while we fed and then I took my turn so he could eat. Nothing else happened thank goodness. But as soon as we had eaten, we went home. Just to be on the safe side. Outside our home on a high branch was Oscar and Olive Owl waiting for us to return. They didn't dare go to either lake at the moment. Just in case they got shot as well. They swooped down onto the lower branches and blurted out that two people with a gun were shooting at anything that moved. They were killing just for the fun of it. Yuk. People are so cruel. Also they had heard from Harold Hare that a family of otters from a lake further into the forest had all been killed, except one who somehow escaped even though she had been shot. No one has seen this otter for twenty-four hours. Probably dead by now they said. "It must be the same two people" said Robbie. They have had their fun by the other lake, so now they have come here. Also pigeon, rabbit and rats lay dead all over the place. We stayed close to home for the rest of the day just to be on the safe side.

Next morning Oscar flew by to say that the big lake seems to be safe at the moment, but two people have been seen near the little lake. So as quick as we could we went to the big lake and had our meal. David and Dorothy Deer and their latest foal were there as well. They were having a drink at the edge of the lake. When all of a sudden they dashed off as fast as they could go. Naturally so did we because, their running so suddenly told us that there was danger about.

As we ran we spotted two people with a gun trying to hide behind some bushes. So we all ran even faster to get to safety. As we arrived at our home we noticed a strange otter hiding nearby. Nigel ran up to her and shouted to us that she was injured. We took her inside and looked at her wound. Luckily for her it was not too bad. A pellet from a gun had grazed her head. It nearly hit her eye, which would have blinded her. Nigel seemed to want to look after her so we decided to let him. We had taught him how to look after his own cuts and grazes. So we were sure that he could look after his new-found friend. Her name was Pauline and she was the otter that escaped with her life. Her family had been killed, her home was not a safe place to go back to so she had nowhere to go. After a family discussion we decided that she could stay here with us if she wanted to do so. She thanked us very much and said that she would love to stay with us. Nigel seemed extra pleased with the decision.

We had to find a way to stop these bad people. What they were doing was against the law. But what could we do? In the forest there are people called Forest Rangers. They are here to look after the forest and us animals that live here. But how do we get them to see what is happening in our part of the forest. There are not a lot of them and the forest is quite big. We had to do something before we all got killed. We had to take a chance and feed where we could. Always leaving two on the lookout while the rest of us fished. Oscar and Olive Owl helped the other birds by staying high in the trees while they fed on the lake. At least being high up it gave them a good view so they could see if there was any danger. David and Dorothy Deer and their foal moved quite a way away to another part of the forest just to be on the safe side. They will come back when it is safe again. That can't be soon enough for us.

The birds on the lake have not long finished making their nests so they will soon have eggs to look after. If the men with their guns are still around they will be in even more danger because they will be sitting on their nests for most of the day. They will literally be sitting targets.

For a few days we did not see them so we hoped that they had gone away. Unfortunately a few days later Oscar and Olive Owls flew over to us and said that they had been feeding further away from the big lake when they saw the men with the gun. They shot at some swans nesting nearby. The swans had been hit in the wings and the legs. The men got to the nest and stole the eggs. Now they were heading our way again. But all the news was not bad. They had seen the Forest Rangers in the area. Apparently they had spotted some of the dead birds and animals and seemed to be trying to find out who had done such bad things. Sam and Sarah Swans now had six eggs and would do anything to protect them. So would Derek and Deirdre Duck because they had four eggs themselves. Both families had their nests on the island on the big lake, so if anyone wants to get to them they will need to get a boat All they need is a small rowing boat because the island is not that far away from the main bank. The nests were amongst the reeds so hopefully they had some protection. But we realised that it would not be long before the men found out just where the nests were. Unfortunately some fishermen had left their little rowing boat on the edge of the lake. Probably because they come down here to fish on most weekends. We found out that the two men with the gun had set up a tent not far from the big lake. As it was getting late we assumed that the two men were staying for a bit longer at least. We warned Sam and Sarah Swan who also told Derek and Deirdre Duck. But there was nothing that they could do. They could only stay and defend their eggs. How could they leave them to be stolen or just broken by the two nasty men. A lot of the other birds had either lost young or had their nests pulled to pieces. They would just have to wait until the two nasty men either left the area or were caught by the Forest Rangers. But how do we help to get them caught. The next morning Oscar and Olive Owl were waiting for us to get up for breakfast. Robbie was first to see them. They told him that the two men were up and that

they were heading towards the big lake. Also they knew that the Forest Rangers were in the area. They were doing a check around the lakes. Perhaps they had seen the dead animals and birds around the area. This means that they will be on the lookout for someone with a gun. We had to find a way to get them to come to the lake when the men were shooting at some of the animals. Even us if necessary. We decided that we needed to get all the birds onto the lake. But of course not on the same side as the two men with the gun. So we got them to land and hide in the reeds and shrubs around the lake near the nests. Oscar and Olive flew off to tell all the birds of our plan.

They could do it so much faster because unlike us they can fly. Oh. How I wish at times that I could fly as well. We told Nigel, Pauline and our other children to stay near our home so they would be safe. Then off went Robbie and myself to see Ratty Rat and Harold Hare. Time was flying by; we had a lot to do if we were going to be ready in time. Oscar flew back to us just as we reached the edge of the lake. The bad men had almost reached the boat. "Are you all ready?" "Nearly!" I said. Just got to get everyone onto the island and into hiding. By the time the bad men had reached the rowing boat, everyone was in their place. All waiting for Oscar and Olive to give the signal. We all waited quietly and patiently until the men were just getting out of the rowing boat. Oscar had asked Katie Kestrel to let him know where the Forest Rangers were. She flew over to Oscar and said that they were only about one hundred and fifty yards away, and hopefully coming towards the big lake. Don't worry said Oscar we will soon attract their attention. The two men were now on the bank and heading for the reeds where the nests were. One of them was carrying the rifle. Good said Robbie. I hope they will get caught with the gun. Just then Olive Owl gave a loud hoot, and all the rats hiding on the edge of the lake swam to the shore and headed in the direction of the Forest Rangers. There must have been at least two hundred rats all running together. Katie Kestrel guided them towards the Forest Rangers.

The two nasty men took no notice of them because they wanted the eggs in the bird's nest. "Plenty of time to shoot the rats later" one man said to the other. The three Forest Rangers could hardly believe their eyes when all the rats ran around them and through their legs. Two hundred rats seemed an awful lot when you see them all running towards you at once. But in a few seconds they had gone past the Rangers and into the forest. They had done their job well. Because the rangers guessed something was wrong, and started walking towards the lake. The two bad men were shouting into the reeds, to try and frighten the birds off of their nest. It did not seem to matter if they injured or killed them. They just did not seem to care. Just then Oscar Owl gave his signal. Two loud hoots. All the geese flew into the air at once. At least forty of them. Katie Kestrel flew past them and shouted, "follow me and keep close." So off they flew behind her. Katie led them towards the Rangers who had just reached the edge of the trees. This was about fifty yards from the lake. While this was going on Robbie and myself with the help of Ratty Rat had been pushing the little rowing boat away from the island and towards the edge of the lake. The three Rangers had seen the geese fly up and now knew for certain that something was very very very wrong on the island. You should have seen the look on their faces when they saw the boat coming towards them. To start with they did not see Ratty Rat or us. I am sure they must have thought that it was moving by itself, until they spotted us. One of them grabbed the end of the boat and held it so that the other two could get into it. Then he got into the boat and then they started to row towards the island. We all swam behind the boat to get back to the others waiting on the island for us.

When we reached the shore we headed for the reeds where all the birds were guarding their nests. They seemed a lot happier now that the Rangers were there. Suddenly just as the bad men were about to shoot Sarah Swan they spotted the Rangers rowing towards them. How did they get the boat said one to the other. They would never believe the truth if you told them, would they. Realising that they had been seen they decided to throw the gun into the lake. If they did not have a gun then they could not be prosecuted for all that had happened. Unfortunately for them the gun landed amongst the reeds. Not in the lake like they wanted. They thought they would be safe because you could not see the gun. It was well hidden by the reeds.

When the Rangers reached them they said that they had just been exploring. There were not any dead birds or animals to be seen so they thought that they were in the clear. In fact they nearly got away with it. Just as the Rangers were about to give up and let the two men go they heard a lot of noise coming from the reeds. So one of them went to investigate. Just then Nigel and Pauline struggled out of the reeds. They were carrying something between them. "Well I'll be blowed" said the Rangers. "Those two otters are carrying a gun. Where on earth did they get that?" Nigel and Pauline dropped the gun on the ground and disappeared back into the reeds. Then they dived into the lake and swam to what they thought was a safe distance away.

The Rangers took the two men away. We have not seen them since thank goodness. I hope that we never do. We seem to be a lot safer now. But of course there is always danger in our lives. The swans and ducks have lovely chicks now.

We thanked all the others for such a lot of help. We could not have done it without everyone's help could we. When we got home Robbie said to Nigel and Pauline that they were naughty for not doing as they were told, which was to stay near our home. But of course they are not babies now. And without their help in recovering the gun the bad men would have got away with the terrible things they had done. So of course we forgave them. Not long afterwards Nigel and Pauline told us that they loved each other and wanted to move to their own home. But not far away I am pleased to say. So next year I will probably be a nanny, I do hope so. Well that's the end of this story. I hope that you enjoyed it. Be good and try to help your mummy and daddy. Just like Nigel and Pauline.

Bye for now.

Sue Kettle.

Mummy Otter.

# CHAPTER SIX

# ONE GOOD TURN
# DESERVES ANOTHER

Hello again children. This is the 6th story about our life in the New Forest. I hope that you enjoy it. My children have grown up now and tend to lead their own lives. But we all live quite close to each other. Nigel has settled down with Pauline about half a mile further along the river. Pauline is the otter that came to live with us when those nasty men with the gun killed her family. Nigel and Pauline seem very happy together. Sometimes they come and feed in the big lake with us. But lately the water has not been coming down the river and into the lake like it should. I am sure it will start again soon. I hope so because we are struggling to catch the amount of fish we need to survive.

On this lovely sunny day just after we had eaten and were resting on the bank of the lake, Oscar and Olive Owl flew down and landed by Robbie's side. They said that they had been feeding deeper in the forest when they came across some New Forest ponies. They seemed very upset, so Oscar called out to them to see what the trouble was. Unfortunately the ponies had been startled when eating the grass on the edge of the forest when some people shouted, screamed and made as much noise as they possible could. This took the ponies by surprise and naturally they ran into the forest. The foals did not run as fast or in the same direction as their parents and got captured by the people. They forced them into their lorries and drove off. The ponies realised too late. The foals had gone.

So the parents started looking all over the forest for their young. But they had not had any luck so far. Oscar and Oliver asked us to help look for them. So we spoke to the birds and all the animals that we thought would assist us. Everyone said of course that they would help. The ducks, swans, geese and all the other birds spread out and flew over the forest to look for the foals. The animals (including us of course) started to search on the ground.

A couple of hours later the swans landed very excitedly on the lake near us. They had found them! They were several miles away in a compound made by the humans. We told Oscar and he immediately flew into the air and headed for the ponies. When he reached them he told them the good news. They got very excited and were soon following Oscar back to us. The swans had told us where the foals were so when the ponies arrived, we led them to their young ones.

"How will they set them free?" said Pauline. "Lets leave it to them" replied Robbie. The ponies looked around the compound until they found the weakest point. Then they turned their backs to the fence and with their powerful back legs they kicked and kicked until part of the fence collapsed. The young foals soon ran back to their parents. Then we all made our way back home knowing that we had helped others. The ponies were very grateful for our help and said that if they could ever help us to just call them. I bet they did not expect to hear from us for some time.

The next morning when we went to feed in the big lake we noticed that the river was still dry. This was bad news for all of us because the river carried food for many of us into the lake. It had been several weeks now and the food was getting very short. Robbie spoke to all the birds and animals that lived on or by the lake. "What can we do?" they all said "First we must find out why" (they all agreed with this) so Oscar flew along the riverbed until he spotted the problem. The river had been dammed with logs. Probably those humans again. They had dammed the narrowest part of the river to help fill a smaller lake.

Not long after we all arrived to see for ourselves. Everyone wondered what we could do. The dam was too well built for any of us to be able to knock it down. Even with our teeth and Ratty Rat's teeth we had no chance. The only other option was to all move our homes to this lake. But we did not want to do that. But what else could we do.

Suddenly Oscar owl came up with a wonderful idea that just might work. He said how about asking the ponies to help us. "Yes! Yes! Yes!" they all shouted. "Let's ask them today." Sam the swan suggested that we all eat here for now while Oscar went to find the ponies and ask for their help.

*...they started kicking with all their might at the dam. Before very long the dam started to fall down and the water rushed in.*

So off went Oscar while we set about finding our lunch. When we had all eaten enough we rested on the bank of the lake while we waited for Oscar to return. Back he came a couple of hours later and told us that the ponies would meet us tomorrow morning.

Early next morning Oscar woke us up to tell us that the ponies were on there way. They had left eight mother ponies to look after their young just in case the men came back. Good idea we all said.

The ponies examined the dam and decided that the only way to remove it was to kick it down. They could do this by standing in the river bed that was dry at the moment. I did point out that they would have to be careful when the water rushed through when they were kicking a hole in the dam. They said it was worth a try because we had helped them so much the other day.

So four of them clambered down into the dry river bed and started kicking with all their might at the dam. Before very long the dam started to fall down and the water rushed in. But fortunately the ponies clambered onto the bank before the water got too high.

Now it was our turn to thank them for all their help. But all they would say was that one good turn deserves another. And if they could ever help again to just give them a call. We thanked them again and all went home.

The humans have not dammed the river for a long time now. Lets hope that they never do again. Selfish people.

# Norman Bailey

Well that the end of another story. I hope you liked it.

Bye for now

Sue Kettle.

Mummy Otter.

# CHAPTER SEVEN

# MISTAKEN IDENTITY

Hello again children. It is raining very hard today and we also have very strong winds here in the New Forest. This sort of weather seems to happen quite a lot nowadays so we just put up with it and get on with our lives the best way we can.

Today I would like to tell you a story about a case of mistaken identity. This can easily happen when people/animals/birds etc are too quick to blame anyone for a problem instead of finding the real culprit. In other words it is a case of the easy option instead of the truth

This is my seventh story about our life in the forest and I hope that you like it.

It seems a long time ago since we got to know the New Forest ponies and had a time of helping each other. These times are always special to us because by helping each other we learn to make new friends. There are good and bad in all types of creatures on this earth. My story of the adder family is a good example. We have not seen that bad family for a long time now. Perhaps they have changed. I do hope so.

Anyway that's enough chitchat. This story tells of how easy it is to blame the wrong creatures for something someone else did.

One autumn day a few years ago, I was fishing in the big lake with Robbie and our children. The new young of ours were doing quite well considering they have had so little experience in catching their own food. I have been catching most of it for them up to now, but it is time they had a go themselves. So lunch took quite a bit longer than usual on this learning day.

By the time everyone was fully fed, both Robbie and myself needed some rest. It is hard work keeping an eye on the children. Especially as they seem to think that chasing the ducks seems more fun than fishing for your own dinner. So as usual but a lot later than expected we laid on the bank of the lake for a rest. We stayed with the children near to us for safety.

This was a very bad year for food. Not just for us but also for quite a few animals in the forest.

While we were resting and trying to keep the children from causing chaos as usual we had a visit from Oscar and Olive Owls. They landed on the ground between Robbie and myself.

"This is not a social call," says Oscar. "There is a lot of trouble brewing. We all know that food is in short supply. Especially meat."

"Well what is the problem?" I said.

Olive started chattering very fast and said that the rabbit family had lost a lot of their young. They just go out to play and never come back. They have just disappeared into thin air. The ducks and moorhens have had a lot of their eggs stolen and I do believe that the Canadian Geese have lost several young chicks as well as a few eggs.

"Something is very dangerously wrong" pipes up Oscar. "Have you seen anything that could help us find the culprit?"

We could not help because we had been too busy looking after our own young lately. But we did agree to keep our eyes well and truly open just in case the culprit struck again. Also we would talk to any other animals and birds we see to see if they had seen anything.

We were very tired so we went to our home and took it in turns to keep an eye on our children just in case they became a target for whoever was doing these bad things.

The next morning bright and early we were on our way to the lake to fish for our breakfast. As usual the children were chasing any animal or bird smaller than they were. Life was mostly a game to them.

Just as we reached the lake and were about to dive in to catch some fish, George Goose charged across the lake and shouted at us. "Why are you here so early? What have you been doing?" He kept on shouting at us until Robbie managed to shut him up for a few moments.

"Now" said Robbie very calmly. "What is the problem and how can we help."

George Goose said that two of his young had slipped out of the nest without Gloria Goose noticing and had disappeared. He even thought for a moment that we had eaten them.

It took a little while to convince him that we eat fish not young geese.

We went back to their nest where Gloria was sitting with the four babies that they had left. They were tucked safely under her wings. Naturally she was very upset because two of her babies were missing. Even we did not think they had any chance of finding them alive.

Just then Sam Swan swam over to us. He was very excited but also a bit scared. Earlier in the morning he had seen a dog type figure lurking on the bank near their nest. It was not light enough to see which animal it was. But he thought it might have been the wild boar that has recently moved into the area. He wanted everyone to get together and chase them away.

I was not happy with this idea because no one had proof that it was the boar family. So I suggested that we all help find out exactly who was doing all these bad things.

We got everyone together as quickly as we could. This was quite easy because most of them live on or near the lake.

Oscar and Olive Owls flew to where the wild boar lived and told them of the meeting. This may seem a silly thing to do considering Sam Swan thought that it was them who were eating the young and the eggs.

Ratty Rat agreed with me that they should be at the meeting. At least we can keep our eyes on them if they are here I said.

Everyone was at the meeting and quite a few suggestions and ideas were discussed. In the end we decided to keep a 24-hour watch all around the lake as this was the area where most of the trouble was. Every family would take it in turns during the night to sleep while others kept watch. This way if there was an intruder we were bound to see it. During the day one of the family would keep a look out while the rest ate. Then someone was on lookout at all times.

Night-time was definitely the most dangerous, as that was when all the animals had disappeared so far.

As soon as anyone saw anything unusual they had to call out as loud as they could. Oscar and Olive Owl would fly over and check to see what the problem was. They even took it in turns to sleep so one of them could be on lookout at all times. They stayed in a big tree on the edge of the lake as Sam Swan saw the creature in this area.

Most of the birds lived and nested here and there were quite a few rabbits nearby as well. So if we were to find out who was doing these bad things we thought this was the best place to watch.

Even the wild boar moved their family into a grassy clearing sheltered by trees on the edge of the lake.

It was in the early hours of the morning that I heard the hoot hoot from the owls. We told our children to stay very still and quiet while Robbie went to find out what was going on. He was halfway to the lake when a large dog type of creature ran past him. Very close behind was Bertie Boar. He did not stop when he saw Robbie. He just kept running as fast as he could. Behind him were two more of his family. One of them stopped when they saw Robbie. "It's a large fox," he said. "That's who has been stealing the eggs and killing the young."

A short time later when the two boars returned they said that the fox had outrun them. But at last we know who the culprit is. They decided to have a meeting with

everyone after breakfast. Now would be a good time to feed, as it is unlikely that the fox will come back today.

A couple of hours later we all met and made sure that there were no more casualties.

Everyone was a bit tired because of all the problems of the last couple of days, so after talking between ourselves we decided that everyone should go home and get some sleep. We would meet a bit later in the day. It is best to discuss such an important matter when everyone was refreshed. Oscar and Olive Owls said they had called a few of their family to keep a look out for us just in case the fox came back before we woke up.

Once again everyone came for the meeting and everyone had a chance to suggest what to do about the fox.

The best suggestion came from Bertie Boars family. If they waited in the tall ferns that surrounded the lake overnight they just might be able to catch him. They would surround the fox but would not hurt him as long as he did not try to escape. I made them promise this, which they did.

That night Bertie and his family did as they said they would and waited in the tall ferns. They had to keep as quiet as they possibly could so the fox would not know they were there. They waited and waited until they thought the fox was not coming. "Perhaps we frightened him off for good" said Bertie. When all of a sudden a rabbit that was feeding nearby suddenly came dashing into the tall ferns where Bertie and his family were waiting.

Perfect thought Bertie. Lets hope the fox is chasing the rabbit. Richard Rabbit had decided the best thing to do was to hide behind one of the boars for safety. Just then the fox dashed into the ferns after the rabbit. He stopped suddenly when he saw the boars. He tried to turn and run the other way but it was too late because the boars surrounded him. He just stood there and said in a very frightened voice "are you going to kill me?"

"Why shouldn't we kill you? You have killed some of our friends. Lets get everyone here and decide what to do with you shall we."

Everyone was wide-awake by now because of all the noise. So we all joined Bertie and his family amongst the ferns. The fox was still surrounded and he still looked very scared and so he should.

We discussed what to do with him, how he should be punished. But the decision would not be an easy one.

The fox steals eggs to eat and he kills other animals for the same reason. But us otters catch fish to eat and the owls eat mice and other small creatures. So all this had to be taken into account when deciding the best punishment. The only difference between us is the fact that the fox sometimes kills a lot more than he can possibly eat. This is killing for the sake of it. The fox must be made to realise that this is wrong.

We took a long time to come to a decision. The other creatures all had their own ideas of punishment, but we all agreed that to kill him would be wrong. This would only make us as bad as him. Our group decision was to banish him to the other side of the forest and never come back. If he did return we would deal with him more harshly. He also promised to catch only enough to eat. We did not know if he would keep to this promise but we decided to give him one chance.

Bertie and his family escorted him to the other side of the forest. The owls flew along to make sure he did not try to escape.

We did not see them until next morning around breakfast time. Everyone was much happier now. George Goose said he was sorry for blaming us otters and Sam Swan said he should never have blamed Bertie and his family.

We were all so glad that this danger was now over and we could all get back to normal again. But I feel sure that everyone had learnt a big lesson. Find out the facts before blaming anyone. Also try to help each other if you possibly can. We do in the forest and it works. So why don't you give it a try?

Well that's all for now children until next time.
Bye for now.

Sue Kettle.

Mummy Otter.

# CHAPTER EIGHT

# BLACK AND DANGEROUS OR JUST AFRAID

Hello again children. If you have read any of my other stories I hope that you enjoyed them.

Today I would like to tell you about two creatures that humans let loose in the New Forest.

This happened a few years ago. At the time I had my hands full with six (yes six) youngsters of my own. I am certainly kept very busy from day break to night-time since they were born. But as they started to grow up they got a bit easier. Robbie was my partner and he gave me as much help with them as he possibly could. He would catch lots of food for them to eat and would look after them when I needed a rest. Our main food is fish. But we do eat frogs sometimes for a change.

Now where was I! Oh yes I remember now. I was about to tell you the story of the two strange creatures that had arrived in the forest.

I was doing the daily task of cleaning the children after they had eaten their dinner. We were on the bank of the big lake where we usually fished for lunch. There were lots of fish for us this year thank goodness. I certainly did not want to have to travel far with these six. As soon as my back is turned to talk to one of them, another one is hiding or up to some mischief. All of a sudden down flew Olive Owl and almost landed on my tail. She seemed to be in a right state. When she started to talk it made no sense at all. Calm down I said to her.

Eventually when she got her breath back she started to tell me the news. I must admit that it did not seem to be good news either.

Apparently Reg and Ruth Rabbit had been feeding in their usual place near their burrow with their young, when from behind one of the bushes by the long grass, out charged a creature and grabbed one of her babies and ran off with the poor thing in its jaws. As soon as the others saw this happen they ran as fast as they could for the safety or their burrows. But as they ran through the bracken, out pounced another one of those creatures and grabbed another rabbit. The rest got home, but those two will never be coming home again.

I know that life can be dangerous for all us animals here in the forest but we have not heard or seen these creatures before. We thanked Olive Owl and off she flew to tell all our friends of the danger. We decided to get the children home as soon as possible. We thought that they would be safer there. On the way we saw Bertie Boar, but he had already been told the bad news. But he had his own ideas about the problem. "Those rabbits get scared of their own shadows" he said." I expect that it was that rotten fox again. Big black creatures indeed. Huh. I will take a couple of my brothers over to their burrows and have a look around. If it is the foxes again we will soon frighten them away. Just leave it to us. As he walked away he muttered under his breath. It sounded like, "blooming rabbits. Its always us helping them. About time they stood up for themselves."

Just to be on the safe side we kept the children very close to our home for the next couple of days. Robbie and I took it in turns to catch the food for our family. One of us fishing and the other on the bank looking out for any danger. Even if Bertie Boar was right and it was the foxes on the hunt, we had to be careful because they could easily carry off one of our babies. They do not usually bother us otters, but if they are very hungry they just might try.

Two days later just as Robbie and I were taking the fish back home for the children, we saw Sam Swan swimming towards us in the lake. "Have you heard the news?" he said shakily. "Two big black creatures have killed a deer not far from here. Even Bertie Boar says it cannot be the foxes this time as the deer are too big for them to kill. "He said that we should be extra careful until we all know just what type of creatures they are. We all agreed with this and headed for home as fast as we could go. We all worried in case our children decided to disobey our instructions and wander outside without us being there to protect them.

Over the next few days we heard stories of different animals being killed and eaten by those two creatures.

Robbie and I agreed that something had to be done to protect us and all our friends The way things were going we would not have any friends left if the killing went on as it was now.

We asked Olive and Oscar Owls to spread the word that there was going to be a meeting the following day by the big lake. Also to say that everyone was invited.

After we had breakfast and cleaned the children (How do they get so messy every mealtime?) we made our way to the big lake. We left the children with the Boar family who often baby-sat for other creatures in emergencies. Oscar Owl had got some of his family perched high in the trees to look out for any danger while the rest of us got to grips with the problem of the two big bad creatures. Bertie Boar had fifteen of his family with him, so we felt quite safe for now.

We were deep in discussion when six New Forest ponies came down to the lake for a drink. When they saw us all together they came over to us. They know that we only get together like this when something is very wrong here in the forest.

The lead pony (Peter) said, "Are you here because of the two black panthers roaming around here?" Of course none of us had ever seen panthers before. At least now we know just what sort of creatures we are dealing with.

Peter told us that they were being taken from an old zoo to be released in a big compound on the other side of the forest. Quite a long way from here. The lorry was involved in an accident and they managed to escape. Until now they have not had to hunt for their own food, because the humans have always been there to give them all they needed. But now they have got to hunt for their own. Also they have not been free before, so they are scared. Even Peter and his family were no match for them. The panthers could easily trap and kill one of them. So the ponies needed the help from all of us just as much as we needed their help.

Bertie Boar and his family said that they could get together and try to chase them away to another part of the forest. But even that would be dangerous for them. Also there was no way to be sure that they would not come back here whenever they got hungry. But what else could we do?

We all decided to go and feed our families and ourselves, have a good think and meet back here the next morning.

After Robbie and I had fed and cleaned the terrible six (that's our nickname for them.) we let them have an hour of exercise before being confined to our home again while Robbie and I went to the meeting. We wanted to make sure they were safe and not going to end up as a dinner for the panthers.

Just as the children were going inside I noticed that we were one short. I had only five not six children with me. I called out to Robbie and he went back along the same path that we had just come down. I took the other five to the safety of our home. I was hoping that our baby had already gone there. But when we went inside we found that our home was empty. I was getting very worried now. Where can he be?

A while later Robbie came home with a very dirty and very tired baby otter in his mouth. I scolded the poor little mite but was so pleased that he was home safe and sound.

"Where was he?" I said to Robbie. "Oh! He found a new badger set and decided to play in the tunnels. (A badger set is where badgers live.) I think Billy Badger frightened him a bit. But he did not really mind him being there. He got Betty Badger to keep him there until they could let us know. But I was passing by and they called me over. I think our little one was pleased to see me. Somehow I do not think he will be doing that again."

We started talking about the panthers and Robbie suggested trapping them so that the humans could take them away to a place where they would be able to live without keeping us in constant fear. But how could we do that. They are much stronger and bigger than any of us.

By the time the next morning arrived Robbie and I had come up with a plan that would involve a lot of the other animals and also a lot of hard work. We would have liked to talk to the panthers and perhaps reason with them. But we knew this would do no good at all. They have not been free before, so they did not know how to behave with other creatures.

My six children were not washed yet because they decided to have an (I do not want to.) day. As we were going to be very busy, I decided to let them get away with it just this once. But I would make up for it at bedtime. A good wash was on the cards for all of them then.

Once again we met by the big lake. A few of the other animals put forward a few good ideas. But some of them would be too dangerous for us to try and might result in a few animals getting themselves killed and eaten. So we decided not to try these ideas. Then they asked Robbie if he could suggest a way to get rid of the panthers. He told them of our discussion last night and they seemed interested.

It would take a lot of hard work from all of us but just might work and there would be less danger to most of us. Billy Badger and his family would play a big part if we were to succeed. He was very excited about the plan and said that his family would love to help.

Our idea was for Billy Badger and his family to dig a big hole. Badgers are very good at digging holes. They are very fast as well. So we knew they would not take too much precious time in getting the job done.

Once the hole was dug we needed some of the other creatures to collect branches, bracken and long grass to cover the hole with. Bertie Boar and his family put the branches across the hole and the other animals covered these with the bracken etc that was collected. A couple of hours later the job was completed. Now all we needed was to find a way to get the panthers to fall into our trap. Also we wanted the Forest Rangers to find them and take them away to safety. We certainly did not want them to die there. The hole had been dug on a road in a quiet part of the forest. This was to make sure that we did not trap the wrong creatures or even humans.

The children seemed to find this more fun than we did. It was just a game to them. But at least they helped as much as they could.

We stopped for lunch and tried to think.of a way to get the panthers here. After we had eaten and rested we went back and met the others by the trap. Everyone had worked very hard and we hoped that the result would make all of the work worthwhile.

Lots of our friends had come back and were eager to

put forward their ideas on how to get the panthers to fall into the hole. But no one had yet come up with an idea on how to get the humans to find the panthers once we had them trapped. Just then Mark the mischievous magpie flew down beside me "this any good to you" he said as he dropped something at my feet. It was a shiny studded collar (broken). "Found it near where the lorry crashed. The lorry that was carrying the panthers through the forest". Before I could speak, his mate flew down and dropped another similar collar at my feet.

"Gosh Mark and Marie, this is just what we need. We will be able to attract the Forest Rangers with these." My children seemed to like the collars because they started running around and chasing each other with them. Robbie soon told them to leave them alone in case they lost them.

Mark had wanted to keep them because they are so shiny and magpies love collecting shiny things. But Marie had convinced him to bring them to us.

"Just give us a call if we can help any more." They shouted as they flew a short distance into the trees. Now the plan was complete. All the animals went and hid. The panthers would be very hungry as they had not eaten for several days. Olive and Oscar had been watching them to make sure they did not wander anywhere near us when we were getting the trap ready. The rabbits all went into their burrows, the birds flew up into the trees and the other creatures hid out of sight.

The senior deer called Dan had volunteered to be the bait for the panthers. He was very brave to do this, as it was a very dangerous task. But we knew that he could run very fast and he knew this part of the forest very well because he fed here most of the time.

Bertie Boar and his family were hiding close bye just in case Dan got caught by the panthers. They would charge in and help him escape if possible. Everything was in place, so now was the time to put our plan into action.

Off went Dan the Deer at top speed. He was by far the fastest of the deer family, but would still need all of his skill and a lot of luck to stay ahead of the panthers. I am sure he was very scared at this moment but he did not show it. I am sure that we were all scared for him as well.

The owls told us where the panthers were. So Dan ran past them at full speed and hoped that they would follow him. As soon as they saw him they gave chase. They were so fast that Olive Owl thought that they would catch Dan before he got to the trap. But he managed to swerve and jump in different directions to keep away from them. Nearer and nearer they came until Dan gave one enormous leap as he reached the trap. I do remember my heart missing a beat because I thought he was going to fall in. But he just about made it to the other side. But as the panthers raced after him they landed on top of the bracken, fell through the thin branches and landed in the bottom of our hole. The trap had worked. The sides were to steep for them to climb up so we were safe for now.

The next step was to get the Forest Rangers to come and collect them. So we called Mark and Marie and asked them for their help.

"What can we do for you?" They chirped. "We are

*The panthers raced after him they landed on top of the bracken, fell through the thin branches and landed in the bottom of our hole. The trap had worked.*

only too pleased to offer our services. It seems that you have all done your share of the hard work."

They listened to our plan and then grabbed one collar each in their beaks before flying off. Oscar Owl had been keeping a look out to see where the Rangers were so that we could get their attention when the time was right. That time was now. Oscar led the two magpies to where the Ranges were and wished them luck. The Rangers were amazed when Mark and Marie both dropped a panther collar in front of them.

Mark said that they looked stunned at first. It is not every day that magpies drop collars at their feet.

Mark landed and picked up one of the collars. He then walked up to one of them and dropped it on his shoe. The Ranger laughed as he bent down to pick it up. Marie did the same to the other Ranger. This seemed to wake them up good and proper. They knew the panthers had escaped and seemed to realise that these were the collars from them. Mark and Marie flew into the lower branches of a nearby tree. Then they started chirping very noisily and very loud. The Rangers seemed to understand what they wanted and started to follow them. Just then one of Dan Deer's family came into the clearing. Just below the tree where the two magpies were standing. "Fly down onto my back." He said. "Then perhaps we can get those two Rangers to follow quicker." So down they flew and perched on the deer's back.

The Rangers had certainly got the idea and sped up to keep pace with the deer. They soon came across the hole with two panthers inside looking sorry for themselves. They did not know for sure how this had all happened but they had a rough idea. Perhaps all the animals and birds looking out from their hideholes had given the game away.

The Rangers called for a lorry to take the panthers away to a safe place. We all felt very sorry for the panthers but we needed a safe home for the rest of us.

The Rangers were looking around for something when Martin Magpie said to me. "Do you think they could be looking for these." The branch he was standing on had both collars hanging from it. The Rangers spotted them but just smiled and said something. Then they walked away back towards where they lived.

Martin and Marie took a collar each as their reward for their help. We think they deserved that.

Well that's all for now children. Just remember that it does not matter who or what you are, helping each other and working together can help not just other people but possibly yourselves as well.
Bye for now.

Sue Kettle.

Mummy Otter.

"HANGING ON FOR DEAR LIFE."

# CHAPTER NINE

# BRAVE FREDDIE FOX

Hello again children. Today I would like to tell you an amazing story that happened a while ago.

Several years ago, with some help from our other animal friends, we sent a nasty tempered fox away with his tail between his legs. He was banished to another part of the forest forever. We certainly did not expect to see him ever again. But forever is a long time.

One day just after a very hard frosty winter's night, Oscar and Olive Owl flew down to the lake just as we arrived to catch some fish for our breakfast.

"Good morning Oscar and Olive." We said cheerfully. "What can we do for you both today?"

Oscar blurts out that there is trouble coming. He said that Freddie Fox is back in the area. They have come to warn the geese, ducks, swans and everyone else to be on the lookout just incase.

We wondered why he had come back to our area. The only reason we could think of was that the winter had been so very long, cold and frosty. Perhaps there was not enough food in his normal hunting area.

Our three children, who are called Pet, Anne and Michael, were almost as big as we were. So we felt that they should be fairly safe from Freddie.

We had our lunch and tried to get the children to rest on the side of the lake for a while to let their dinner go down. But as usual they wanted to play not rest. Sam the Swan swam by and said that his young were just the same. They do not ever seem to get tired. He had heard about the fox being around. So he got all of his family and took them to the island in the middle of the lake for safety. When he got there he noticed that a lot of the other birds had done the same.

There was Deirdre Duck with her eight large chicks. All of the local geese had moved onto the island as well. So it seemed a bit crowded at the moment.

By the time we had eaten lunch we decided to move to a smaller lake, as the noise from all the birds on the island was terrible. They all seemed to be shouting and squawking at the same time. It is a wonder that anyone could hear at all with that racket going on.

The children were supposed to rest after we had eaten. But as usual they wanted to play. Robbie was cleaning himself and I must have dozed off for a while. When I woke up, I called to Robbie to get the children together, as it was time to go home. Robbie had dozed off as well, so when Pete and Anne answered his call and came running to us. I said. "Where is Michael?" They had not seen him for some time. We called again but still there was no answer from Michael. He was nowhere to be seen.

I took the children home while Robbie went to look for him. When he came home later without Michael I was very worried. He had never gone off alone before.

Just then Olive and Oscar Owls called to us from a tree near our home. They said that Bertie Boar and his family had some news for us. "We think that they have found him." They chirped happily. So off we ran as fast as we could go. We soon reached Bertie Boars home. We certainly had quite a surprise when we heard just what had happened. Bertie and his family had seen Freddie Fox running along at top speed with Michael in his mouth. He was having difficulty running because Michael was no baby now.

So Bertie and his family managed to surround him and make him stop and put Michael down. They were just about to punish him when Michael began to say, "Leave him alone. He was helping me." Bertie Boar thought Freddie Fox was trying to have Michael for his dinner.

Michael explained that he had hurt his leg while running away from some humans with a gun. Freddie saw what was happening and thought they were going to kill him. So he ran over, picked him up and ran with him before the humans could shoot him. Then he just ran as fast as he could until the Boar family stopped him.

Of course when Michael explained all this, we thanked Freddie very much. To show how grateful we were, Robbie dived into the nearest lake and caught Freddie a couple of fish for his supper. He ate them eagerly. He had not had much to eat for a couple of days so he was very grateful for the gesture.

When he had finished his meal, we asked him why

he was so far from his home. He told us that some humans on horses, followed by lots of dogs had chased him for miles. He had been with his mate Freda at the time and had tried to get them to follow him so that she could get away. But they had split up and were following them both. Freda had gone off in a different direction and he could not find her now. He was so worried about her.

We suggested that he stay overnight with Bertie Boar and his family. He should be safe there. Oscar and Olive Owls spoke to their friends and they said that they would keep a look out for her during the night. Freddie was very grateful for all of our help.

Next morning we went to see Freddie and to find out if there was any news about Freda. Oscar and Olive Owls and their friends had been looking for her all night long. Fortunately they had spotted her in a small cave not too far away. Unfortunately the cave was quite near where the humans and the dogs were staying. If she came out of the cave during the daylight, she was sure to be seen. So we got together with Bertie Boar and his family and came up with a plan that just might help rescue her.

One of Bertie's brothers had managed to get some food to her during the night and told her to stay put until she heard from him again.

Just as it was getting dark again, Bertie told about thirty of his family to form a line between Freda and the place where the men and dogs were staying. They had just got into line when the dogs started barking and howling at the top of their voices. This alerted the humans who let the dogs out of the kennels. Of course the dogs headed towards the Boar family. But not for long! The Boars charged towards the dogs, howling as they went. This startled the dogs very badly as they are used to creatures running away, not towards them. So the dogs turned around and started to run the other way. No matter how much the humans shouted at them they just kept on running. The Boars chased them for quite a while to make sure that Freda had enough time to escape.

As soon as the Boars charged the dogs, Freda was told to run. "Follow me." Shouted Robbie at the top of his voice. She followed him for about half a mile. "This should be far enough." Said Robbie. "You should be safe enough here."

Just then Freddie came along and you should have seen the look on his face. He was so pleased and excited all at the same time. "I did not think I would ever see you again." He said excitedly.

They stayed with the Boar family overnight just in case the humans and dogs came back again. But fortunately they did not. They were probably still trying to catch all of those dogs.

In the morning we thanked Freddie once again for saving Michael from the men with the gun. We could have lost him for good if Freddie had not been so quick. Michael gave Freddie a big hug and said thanks.

Now it was time for Freddie and Freda to make their way back to their home on the other side of the forest. We all said our good-byes and thanks and off they went. Perhaps we will meet them again one day. Only next time lets hope that there is no danger involved for any of us.

Well that's all for this time. Just remember to be nice and to help one another when you can.
Bye for now.

Sue Kettle.

Mummy Otter.

"WHO ARE YOU?"

# CHAPTER TEN

# DANGEROUS ANIMALS OR ARE HUMANS TO BLAME?

Hello again children. I am Sue Kettle. I am a Water Otter and I live in the New Forest with my partner Robbie and our four children.

I remember this story very clearly because of how close I came to losing my mate for good.

We had been feeding in the big lake and were on our way home when all of a sudden out of the bush came two male humans.

We heard one of them shout, but not at us. Then we saw two dogs running in our direction. The humans had told them to get us.

Robbie shouted to me to get our children home if I could. He was going to try to to hold them off so that we could get away. So I shouted to the children to follow me and ran like the wind with my children close behind.

I only had chance for a quick look back but I could tell from Robbie's squeals that he was being hurt. There was nothing that I could do to help him. I had to get our children to a safe place first.

Somehow we got home safely and I made sure that our four babies were well hidden just in case the humans or their dogs followed us.

It seemed like hours before I dared to venture out and try to find Robbie.

When I reached the place where we were attacked all I found was a lot of blood on the ground. There was no sign of my Robbie. I did not know what to do and I was so worried about him.

Just then my friend Oscar Owl called out to me. He was sitting in a tree near to us.

"I saw what happened" he said. "But don't worry because Bertie Boar came along just as you were getting your children to safety. It is a good job he did because those two dogs would have killed Robbie."

"He is hurt but I do not know how bad. Bertie Boar held the dogs off so that Robbie could get away. But he did not follow you home in case they followed him. He has gone to Bertie Boars home. He will be safe there" said Oscar. I rushed home to tell our children the news because they were as worried about their dad as I was.

I told them that I was going to see him but they were to stay here and not come out until I came back. I just had to go and see if he was badly hurt.

When I got to Bertie Boars home I found Robbie laying in a safe place protected by Berties family. He was badly bitten but was going to be all right if he rested for a few days.

I knew that he would not be able to fish for food for a few days until he was a bit better. This meant a lot of extra work for me but I did not mind as long as he was going to be all right.

He decided to stay where he was until the next day, so later I took him some supper after I had fed the children. He was already looking more rested thank goodness. But he did look a sorry sight with dog teeth marks all over the place. Bertie said that Robbie had bitten the dogs as well but was definitely losing the fight when he arrived.

Bertie frightened the dogs away and ran at the humans but they were already running away as fast as they could.

A few days later Robbie was feeling much better. He was still sore and bruised but at least he was able to fish for his own food again. This made it easier for me as I still had the children to fish for.

About a week after the attack we were resting on the bank after fishing in the big lake when David and Dorothy Deer came bounding towards us.

"Quickly run and hide" they shouted. "It's the two humans with the dogs again." So as quick as a flash we disappeared into the lake. We knew that they could not catch us there because we were too fast for them in the water. David and Dorothy were running and leaping away from the dogs as fast as they possibly could.

Just then the bushes parted and out ran a rabbit with the two dogs close behind. Within seconds one of the dogs had the rabbit in its jaws. Then the other one grabbed a leg and they started shaking and pulling the rabbit apart. The poor rabbit had no chance and soon died. The two humans just picked up the dead rabbit and laughed as they threw it into the lake. Then they turned around and walked away with the dogs close behind them. So we got out of the lake and headed for the safety of our home.

On the way Bertie Boar and his partner stopped us. Oscar Owl had followed the humans and had found where they lived. He had been asked to do so by Bertie. Also he said that the two dogs were kept in a kennel outside in the garden when they were not out walking.

Bertie suggested attacking the dogs to stop them attacking us smaller creatures but I certainly did not agree with this idea. The humans could soon get and train more dogs to do the same. What we had to do was to get the dogs to help us frighten the humans. Then they would not attack us any more.

After much thought we came up with what we thought was a good idea. Robbie and Bertie were to go and talk to the dogs when the humans were not about. So later that day they crept up to the gate of the humans' home and talked to the two dogs. I was going to go but Robbie said it would be best if I stayed and looked after the children. I thought the dogs might call the humans and tell them that Bertie and Robbie were there but they did not. I think that they were afraid of Bertie and that is why they decided to help us.

Several days later Oscar Owl flew over to us and said that the humans and the two dogs were heading towards the big lake which is exactly where we were. So now was the time to put our plan into action.

When the dogs were 100 yards from us Robbie ran into the open so that they could see him. The humans shouted to the dogs to get him. Off they chased through the bushes after him. As soon as they were out of site of the humans they stopped and so did Robbie. They stood on the edge of the lake and waited.

Very soon we heard shouting. Then we saw the humans come running through the bushes towards us. Behind them, snorting and snarling came Bertie and some of his family. They did not get too close because they only wanted to frighten them a bit not to kill them.

The humans shouted to the dogs to help them. But all they did was wag their tails and give a couple of playful barks as though they thought it was a game.

Bertie Boar and his family chased them all the way to their home on the edge of the forest. When the humans reached the gate to their house Bertie and his family turned around and came back to where we were waiting.

We thanked the dogs for playing along with the trick and everyone else for all their help as well.

The dogs ran off back to the humans and hoped they would not get told off for not helping them.

"We should all be a lot safer now" said Bertie. "I don't think they will be bothering us again." We would be lost without friends like him.

The humans never came back into the forest again but the dogs did come to the lake to see us sometimes.

Well that's all for now children until next time. Just remember that it is nice to help someone when they are in trouble. So remember that for another time.

Sue Kettle.

Mummy Otter.

# CHAPTER ELEVEN

# HELP THEY HAVE TRAPPED ROBBIE

Hello children. Today I would like to tell you about one of the most frightening times of my life. My partner Robbie has always been very good to me and the children that we thankfully have every year. He always helps me to bring them up. He helps me to feed them and also helps to teach them so much as they grow older.

This almost changed forever, but thanks to our many good friends things got back to normal. Or at least as normal as possible.

One day a few years ago, Robbie and myself took our four youngsters to the big lake as usual to have breakfast. We did not notice anything unusual except perhaps that it was quieter than usual. Our four were of course not at all quiet. They had not been up long so they were full of life and wanted to play. I just do not know where they get all their energy. They wanted to play tag or chase the tail. Catching breakfast seemed to be the furthest thing from their minds at this moment in time.

We did not even notice that there were no birds on the lake. Usually at this time of the day there are swans, ducks, geese and numerous other birds around. But we were too occupied with our children to notice today. Robbie was going to try to teach the youngsters to catch fish today but decided to catch his own first.

Robbie dived into the water while I stayed on the bank to keep my eye on the children while they played. They had decided on catch the tail this time. Fortunately my tail was not the one to be caught. But two of them got bored and decided to follow their father into the lake just in case they could share his breakfast.

They soon found him, as they knew where he usually started to look for the fish. They were becoming very good swimmers, which is essential for us otters as we spend a lot of time in the water.

All of a sudden the two children that were following Robbie came to the surface and started to swim towards me. They were trying to shout at the same time but I could not understand a word that they were saying.

When they reached me on the bank of the lake I managed to calm them down enough to make sense of what they were saying.

"Daddy has been trapped, daddy has been trapped" they kept saying.

Just then from amongst the bushes out came three humans. They walked along the bank until they were level with the place where Robbie usually fishes. They bent down and started to pull on some rope that was attached to a tree near the waters edge.

In no time at all I realised that the rope was attached to a trap. As they pulled the trap nearer to the bank and out of the water I saw to my horror that Robbie was inside it. He was shouting to me to take the children to safety. "Just run, run, run and do not look back" he shouted.

I did not want to leave him but I knew that he was right. Also the children were very scared. They clung on to me so tightly that it made me realise that I had to get them to safety as quickly as possible. There could be other humans around waiting to catch us as well. So I told the four of them that we had to run home as fast as possible. Just before we ran I shouted to Robbie that I would get help as soon as I possibly could.

He knew that my first concern had to be our children. So he did not really expect me to be able to cope with them as well as try to help him escape. But I knew that I would never give up. We have been together for a long time now and I was not going to let those nasty humans keep us apart. At that moment in time I had no idea how I was going to help him escape. But I did know that I would never stop trying.

Just as we arrived home I spotted Martin the Magpie on top of our roof. He flew down and said he tried to catch us before we went to the lake. Humans had been spotted putting traps all around and in the lake and so he was trying to tell all the creatures that go there to beware. Unfortunately he got to our home too late. We had already gone. He tried to catch us before we got there but failed, as he had to stop and tell some other animals on the way.

Olive and Oscar owls had been watching them for

some time. They had laid lots of traps for the rabbits and other traps for the ducks, geese and swans. They had asked Martin to help them tell everyone as soon as possible.

"Where is Robbie" asked Martin suddenly? I just burst into tears as I told him that the humans had trapped him. I was too distressed to be of any use at the moment so I took the children inside to safety.

Martin said that he would have a word with a few of our friends straight away and see if there was anything that could be done to help Robbie.

The children were frightened that I would leave them alone. So I told them not to worry, as I would always be there for them.

Martin Magpie met up with a few of his friends and decided to try to help us. They flew to the lake where Robbie got captured in the hope that he was still there. As luck would have it the humans had not left yet. They seemed to be waiting in the hope that some of the other creatures would be caught in their traps. Fortunately just about all of the other creatures had now been warned in time. So everyone was staying away from the lake. There was not a creature in sight. If only we had not been so otherwise occupied earlier, we might have realised that it was too quiet there.

Oscar and Olive met the Magpie family in the forest away from the lake. They had heard the bad news and wondered if there was any way that they could help.

Just then a flock of sparrows flew down and told them that the humans were loading my Robbie and the trap onto a lorry.

*As they pulled the trap nearer to the bank and out of the water I saw to my horror that Robbie was inside it.*

"Right" said Martin. "We must follow them and see where they are taking him. Then perhaps we can try to rescue the poor chap." They all flew to the lake just as the lorry started to pull away. I wonder what they would have thought if they could see the strange crowd following them. There were owls, magpies, sparrows and several other birds all wanting to help.

A couple of hours later the truck stopped. Martin Magpie recognized the place straight away. It was an animal sanctuary on the far side of the forest.

The humans kept all sorts of creatures here and they let lots of other humans come here to look at them. How awful. Why can't they just leave us to be free? We never do humans any harm.

After the birds had seen Robbie and the trap pulled from the lorry they knew that they could do no more today. So they all headed for home. All that is except Oscar owl. He stayed just to make sure that the humans did not move Robbie anywhere else.

Martin came and told me all the news hoping that I would not worry too much. He was such a good friend. When the children saw him they got very excited. Where is daddy? When is he coming home? Is he hurt and lots more questions? Poor Martin did not have much good news for them at the moment. I think he felt awful when he saw their faces drop as he told them that Robbie was not coming home yet. But he did help me quieten them down a lot.

The next morning when I was getting the children ready to go and catch our breakfast, Olive Owl flew down and said that a lot of the forest creatures were going to have a meeting to discuss ways of freeing

Robbie from the sanctuary that was Robbie's prison. So I got the children together and followed Olive Owl to meet the others.

First I needed to get some food for the children and of course for myself. It would be difficult without Robbie here, as I could not look after the children as well as catch the fish for us all.

Just then along came Bertie Boar to see if there was any new news. Unfortunately there was nothing new for me to tell him. As he was just about to go I asked him to do me a favour. I wanted him to look after my four until I caught enough food for us all. He was only too pleased to help. I wondered if he would be so eager another time because when I eventually came back onto the bank he seemed to be very stressed. "What is the matter?" I said to him. "They have been chasing my tail and I am worn out. If I did not run they got upset. So I ran and ran while they chased me. Now I am worn out completely." He said sorrowfully. I had forgotten that boar children do not play in the same way as my otter children. Poor Bertie.

When my little ones had eaten I gave them a good wash. Tim (the eldest. Just.) Tried to get out of being washed. Typical children. When his turn came he pushed one of his brothers forward and said, "it's your turn Reg." But I knew that I had already washed Reg so I got hold of Tim and gave him a good long wash. Perhaps next time he will not try to be so clever. Children do try some different tricks don't they?

When we had all eaten and washed we met to see if anyone had any ideas on how to rescue Robbie.

"First of all we need to go and have a good look at

this sanctuary," blurted Bertie Boar, "then perhaps we will know if it is possible to rescue him." "I think that a few of us should go as we can then put our ideas together. What do you all think of that then."

Everyone agreed that this was a good idea. So Bertie asked for volunteers to go with him. Everyone seemed to want to go. So I suggested that six different creatures went along this time.

Bertie Boar picked out six different creatures and off we all went to the other side of the forest to see for ourselves what the sanctuary was like.

We must have looked an odd bunch all-walking along together. There was Bertie of course and myself with Brenda Badger, Dorothy Deer, Ringo Rabbit and Freddie Fox. Some of the birds flew along to show us the way.

Bertie Boars family had volunteered to look after my youngsters until we came back. I made them promise to be good and not to expect the other creatures to keep playing games with them. They sure have a lot of energy between the four of them. No wonder I get so tired sometimes.

Martin was in the lead showing us all the way. Some of the other birds just wanted us to know that they were there to help if they could.

When we arrived at the compound Martin flew down and told Robbie that we were all there. There were two fences between us. So we could not get as close as we would have liked to. But at least Robbie knew that we were there.

I stood on my back legs and shouted to him. He stood on his back legs as well and we could just see each other's heads. There was a lot of bracken in between the fences making it impossible to see any more than that. I told him that we were there to try and set him free.

Just then I heard some dogs barking furiously. They charged towards us but fortunately they were the other side of the fence so they could not get to us. Bertie said that if they did get out he thought that he could handle them with some help from the others. Good old Bertie.

Brenda Badger said that she could dig a hole under the outside fence quite easily. But if she went all the way through the dogs might get her. Ringo Rabbit sprang over our heads and landed in front of us. "I have an idea." He said very excitedly. "What if the old badger thing dug almost all the way through and then me and my missus dug the rest of the way. Then we could bound over to the other fence and dig a hole between us. We would make it big enough for the Bertie chap to get through. What do you say to that old chap?" Of course we would need the bird types to fly into the trees in the middle of the two fences to keep a look-out for the dogs. They would just love to get their teeth into us. Make a nice supper for them we would that."

We decided to go home and finalize the plan and come back the next day. Plus we all needed to get some food and then as much sleep as we possibly could. We wanted to be fresh for tomorrow. Also I was missing my children very much. I did hope that they were behaving for the Boar family. I do know just how mischievous they can be.

The next morning we set off for the sanctuary. Only today there were more of us. Bertie Boar had brought a few of his family along just in case we needed any help.

If the dogs did get out they would be in lots of trouble with the Boars. Also Brenda Badger had got her partner to come as well. The two of them could dig a nice big hole our side of the fence. This would make it easier for them all to get through. Especially if on the way back they were in a hurry.

When we arrived there Martin had already told Robbie the plan. He was very excited and was at the fence waiting for us.

Brenda Badger and her partner started digging straight away. We did not want to waste any more time. Martin Magpie flew into the trees with some of his family. They spread out around the compound so that they had a good view. If the dogs came along they would call out and let us know straight away.

The Badgers soon dug under the fence and only stopped when they were a few inches from the surface on the other side. Now it was up to the rabbits to dig the rest of the way. They soon dug through and popped out the other side of the fence. They bounded across the ground until they came to the bracken near the other fence. Then they leaped into it and froze because just then the Magpies called out that the dogs were coming. If they found the rabbits they would attack and kill them.

One of the dogs found the holes that the rabbits came through and started digging at them. As soon as their paws went through about six inches, the badgers were waiting for them and struck their paws with their very sharp claws. The dogs soon jumped back in fright and ran away very fast.

Now the rabbits dug as fast as they could. Before

long they were through and came face to face with Robbie. He was so excited to see them that they had a job to calm him down. They told him to follow them through the hole. As soon as they popped their heads out the other side they heard the magpies call out that the coast was clear. So they ran through the bracken out into the clearing. Just as they started to cross they heard the magpies call out. "Watch out the dogs are coming back."

It was too late to turn back so they made a dash for the other hole and freedom. They just managed to get into the much bigger hole that the badgers had made for them when they could feel the breath of the dogs on their back legs. This made them go even faster. Once they were through they saw the Badgers and Boars waiting for them. Just keep running they told them. We will deal with the dogs.

So we did as we were told and kept running as fast as we could. The Magpies were overhead leading the way. When the dogs came through the hole they found that there was a warm reception waiting for them. The Boars and the Badgers pounced on them and chased them back through the hole into the compound. Then they filled the hole back up so that they could not come through again. Then they followed us back home.

Robbie was so pleased to see our children again and I know that there were excited to see their dad back home safely.

When everyone got home we went to see them all and thanked them very much for all the marvellous help that they had given us.

The Boars said that they did not know that children had so much energy but still enjoyed looking after our four. They also told us that they had all learnt to play the new games. They now enjoyed a game of tag and chase the tail.

That's all for now children. But just remember that helping others is always a good way to live your life. Just remember that you may need some help yourself one day. As we did on this occasion.

Goodbye now.

Sue Kettle.

Mummy Otter.

" SAVING THE TEDDY."

# CHAPTER TWELVE

# PLEASE SAVE MY TEDDY

Hello children. Today I would like to tell you another story about our lives in The New Forest. There are six of us at the moment. Robbie is my partner and we have four lovely children.

One sunny summer's day we were taking the children for a walk to a new lake that Robbie had found. We were going to see if there were many fish that we could catch for our dinner.

The lake was at the bottom of a steep hill and was surrounded by trees. These would give us some protection from danger while we were feeding.

Robbie said that he would dive in first to see if there were plenty for us to catch. So I told the children to lay in the sunshine and rest for a while. If only they knew the meaning of the word "rest." As usual they decided to play. This time the game was called pulling a tail. This involves one of them pulling someone's tail and running away. Then the person to whom the tail belonged had to chase the others and do the same to one of them. They made sure that I joined in as well. So I did not get much rest.

By the time Robbie came out of the lake I was exhausted. So Robbie took the children into the lake to fish for their dinner. I stayed on the bank in the sunshine keeping a lookout for any danger. When they had finished it was my turn to fish. Afterwards we went for a walk to the top of the hill to show the children the lovely view. We could see quite a long way from up there.

We had not been there for very long before Robbie shouted to us to hide quickly as danger was approaching. The children followed me into an area of long grass and tall ferns. Robbie was close behind us.

Just then a car came into view and stopped about twenty feet from us. An older man got out from the driver's side and went around to the passenger's door. When he opened the door a little girl got out. She was clutching an old teddy bear close to her. The older man told her to leave the teddy on the seat but she would not let go of it.

The man went to the boot of the car and got out a rug. He placed this on the ground and then pulled a basket from the car. When he opened this I saw food and drink inside. They were going to have a picnic. How wonderful.

We were very pleased that it was not a car full of hunters. They come here sometimes and shoot and trap our friends. They even shoot at us sometimes. Humans can be so cruel.

The little girl called the man "Grandpa." What a lovely name. He called her Emma. "How sweet." I thought. They sat and ate and drank for some time while we watched from our hiding place. Emma seemed to go on talking forever. Constant chatter chatter. This reminded me of my four youngsters.

Sometime later Grandpa put the rubbish in the box and placed it back in the car. Then he started to fold up the blanket. As he was doing this he noticed that Emma was dangerously near to the edge of the hilltop. He shouted to her to get back. At the same time he was running towards her with the blanket in his hands. Unfortunately his foot caught in the blanket and he toppled forward, just missing Emma as he fell. He toppled over the edge of the steep hill and rolled and rolled until a small tree stopped him. Emma was getting nearer and nearer to the edge to try and see her Grandpa. The edge of the hill crumbled away and she also fell. Her teddy bear went one way and she went the other. Fortunately she did not fall very far down the hill.

Robbie ran down the hill to see if he could help at all. He ran past Emma and stopped on the hillside just below her. When she saw him she scrambled to her feet as quickly as she could and clambered up to the top of the hill. She seemed very frightened. She ran back to the car as fast as her legs would carry her. She opened the door, got in and shut the door securely behind her. At least she was safe for now.

I told my children to stay near the car so that Emma could see them. This might just make her stay where she was.

Robbie ran down the hill to see how Grandpa was. When he came back he told us that he thought Grandpa

*Grandpa might have broken his leg. It was bent at an awful angle and needed attention as soon as possible.*

might have broken his leg. It was bent at an awful angle and needed attention as soon as possible.

I went over to where the teddy bear had fallen and took him to Robbie. He had a plan that should help them. He picked the teddy bear up in his mouth and ran off. Robbie knew that there was a bridle path nearby. The local riding school often came this way.

Very soon the ponies and their riders came along. Robbie stepped out in front of them and dropped the teddy bear on the ground. The riders looked amazed and confused. So Robbie started to jump up and down and turn around in circles. But the humans did not seem to understand what he wanted.

The lead pony asked Robbie what the problem was. The humans could not understand him but the ponies could. Thank goodness for that. They promised to follow him if he did not go too fast. "What about the riders. They will not understand why you will not do as they want you to. They will try to keep you going the way they want." Said Robbie.

"Do not worry about them. I will make sure that we follow you. Just leave them to me." He snorted.

So off trotted Robbie with the ponies close behind. The riders tried to make them go another way, but they just kept following him. Eventually they gave up trying and let the ponies go the way they wanted.

Very soon they came to the car where Emma was sitting very still and very frightened.

I told my children to follow me back to the tall grass and ferns. We had to keep out of the way so the humans could help Emma and Grandpa. Emma would soon tell them what had happened and where to find Grandpa.

Two of the humans went down the hill and helped Grandpa, while one of the others went to fetch help.

Very soon Grandpa was on his way to hospital in an ambulance and Emma's mum and dad had been called. They arrived not long after and were very glad to see that Emma was ok.

"Let's go home now." Said Emma's parents. Then suddenly Emma realised that she did not have her teddy bear. Mum and dad looked around for him, but could not see him anywhere.

Just then Olive Owl flew down to me and said. "I think Oscar has something for you." Then Oscar flew down with teddy in his claws. They had been watching Robbie and when he dropped the teddy they waited until the ponies had passed and picked him up. Then they followed them back here. They are so thoughtful.

Robbie picked up the teddy in his mouth and ran to Emma's dad. The look on his face when Robbie dropped the teddy at his feet. He was so surprised that he could not speak.

They will never be able to understand what really happened today. Will they. Even if they tell their friends I should not think that they would believe them. Would you?

Well that's all for today children.

But do remember to be careful and also to help one another when you can. You may need help yourself one day.

Bye for now.

Sue Kettle.

Mummy Otter.

# CHAPTER THIRTEEN

## THE ADDER STORY
## THE ANIMALS FIGHT BACK

Hello again children. Today I would like to tell you about a very scary time that happened a couple of years ago.

I have been very lucky so far because I have always lived in a lovely part of the New Forest. Robby left his parents when he was old enough to look after himself and ended up in my area. That is how we first met.

As we have lived here so long now we have got to know most of the other local creatures in and around the area. We get on well with each other most of the time.

One day when I woke I thought that I could smell burning wood. So I quickly ran outside to investigate. Oscar the Owl was flying by and told me that there had been a forest fire about five miles away. It was blowing the other way at the moment so we were not in any immediate danger. Of course it would pay us to keep our eyes open just in case the wind changed direction.

Careless people could have started the fire in many ways but usually they drop cigarette ends without putting them out and sometimes even light fires in places where they should not. People can be so stupid at times.

By now the rest of my family were awake and ready to go and get some breakfast. I told them about the fire so that they would also keep a sharp look out. So off we went to the big lakes as we knew that there were loads of fish for us to eat.

I spotted Dorothy Deer and her foal having a drink on the edge of the lake so I stopped to see how her young one was getting along. He seemed to be getting quite big considering he was so young. "You have a lovely young one there" I said.

"He is quite a handful" she replied.

Just then her partner came out of the tall ferns. "Hi Sue how are you and the family?" We chatted for a couple of minutes about the young and then I mentioned the fire. Of course they already knew about it. They have very sensitive nostrils and can smell most things before anyone else. Then she said something that sent a shiver down my spine. The part of the forest that was burning was where the nasty Adder family live. We wondered where they would move to now that their homeland was burning.

Just then Olive Owl landed on a branch of a tree near where we were standing. She wanted to know if we had seen Oscar. I told her that I saw him near our home earlier. She thanked me and then just as she was about to fly away to look for him, she said that as she flew over the forest away from the flames, but towards the big lake. She spotted Bob the adder and his family slithering across a grassy clearing. The bad news is that he is coming our way. Then off she flew to find Oscar.

We hoped that the Adders would pass us by and live somewhere else. So we waited and watched. The next day I woke as usual and got the children up and ready for breakfast. Off we went as usual to the big lake, but this time we kept an extra lookout for that nasty family of Adders. When we got there we spoke to all the other animals that had arrived earlier. So far no one had seen them. No sign of Bad Tempered Bob and his family. What good news this was. Perhaps they had passed us by overnight. I do hope so.

As Robbie was feeding I kept my eyes on the youngsters. They seem to have mastered the art of catching fish to eat. This helps me because to start with I have had to fish for them. I had enough to eat and laid down on the bank with the rest of the family to let our food go down. Just then I noticed a group of people coming down the path towards us. Up I jumped and headed for the lake. All the others followed close behind. The children can tell by our behaviour when we think that danger is about.

Nearly all the people that come down to the lake (except the fishermen) bring bread to feed the ducks, swans and other birds that live here. The ducks must have spotted them first because they started paddling towards the shore. They made lots of noise as well. The people threw bread into the lake and then it was a free for all. Every one of the birds on the lake was fighting to get their share of the food. The geese peck each other to try to get them to drop their mouthful. They are so spiteful to each other. The swans just use their size and knock everyone else out of the way. The ducks and moorhens just dart in between them all and pick up whatever pieces they can. It really is fun to watch.

When all the bread had been thrown into the lake the people started to walk away. They decided not to follow the path but to take a short cut across the long grass. All of a sudden we heard the people scream and as we looked up we saw them run out of the grass and back along the path. When they shouted "look out snakes" we knew we had trouble on our hands. It just had to be the nasty Adder Family.

Oscar and Olive Owls flew low over the grass where the people ran from. Then they flew over to us. The news was not good. As we expected it was Bad Tempered Bob and his family. They were watching us from the long grass. The ducks, swans, geese and the other birds got back to their nests as fast as they could. They had to protect their eggs in the best way that they could. Robbie called to our children to follow him and we made our way back to our home. "What are we going to do now" I said to Robbie? We had a long chat about this because we know just how dangerous the nasty Adders are. Normally adders just live their own lives and do not bother us too much. But not this family! They are always bad tempered.

We decided to talk to the other animals and birds as soon as we could. So next morning we had just got up and were getting ready to talk to the other creatures when Oscar flew down to us. During the night the Bad tempered Bob and his family had attacked the nest of Max and Mary Moorhen. They tried to defend their eggs but the snakes had broken them all. The ducks were worried because they expected to be the next to get attacked. They were sure that it would not take the snakes long to find their nest. The swans are much bigger but even they knew that their eggs were at risk. Perhaps they would attack our home as well. But what can we do.

We asked Oscar and Olive to tell everyone that we would like to meet them all at the little lake in a couple of hour's time. We also sent a message to Max and Mary to say how sorry we were about their eggs being smashed.

Everyone turned up with the exception of Derek and Deirdre Ducks who needed to protect their nest. Even Dave and Dorothy Deer and their foal joined us. They graze in the grass so they were very worried about being surprised by the nasty snakes .One bite could kill their baby.

We talked about a lot of different ways to frighten them away but no one came up with an idea that we thought might work. What we needed was someone that could be as nasty as the adders themselves. Individually we could not do much. We otters could bite their tails and hope that they would not bite us. The birds could peck them and hope for the best. The deer could kick them but as individuals we would not succeed.

Just as the meeting was about to end without a solution to the problem, who should pop his head out of a hole in the bank of the lake but Ratty Rat? "Perhaps I can help," he said. Now this surprised everyone because none of us have much to do with the rats and they leave us all alone. It has always been this way in the forest.

"How can you help us?" I said? "Also why should we

trust you." " Well its like this" says Ratty. Nasty Bob and his family of snakes have started slithering into our homes and threatening our families. They have already killed 6 of our babies and we do not want to risk any more of our families. Lets go away for a while and think hard until we come up with a solution to this problem. But we have got to stick together I said. Everyone agreed with this. If we do not beat them we will all have to leave and find new homes. This was not what any of us wanted.

We all got on with the usual things like finding food, cleaning ourselves and of course looking after the children. Plus we had to keep our eyes peeled just in case the snakes came near us. Olive and Oscar dropped food on the ducks nest so that they could stay with their eggs. This would make it harder for the snakes to find out just where their nests are.

By the time evening came and everyone except the ducks crowded onto the little lake we had a plan. The rats have sharp teeth and so had we! So we are the ones who must attack them. All the birds would help protect the nests, the young chicks and eggs. As there are quite a lot of them it may make the snakes stay away. Of course the rats and us otters knew that if we got bitten we might die. But that is a chance that we had to take.

Next morning very early as arranged, we crept quietly towards the long grass where Bob and his family slept. Oscar and Olive owls flew over the grass and hooted when they spotted the snakes.

The attack started with Ratty Rat and a lot of other rats charging into the grass and biting the snakes as hard as they could. Then they ran back past us as we crouched in the grass. The snakes slithered after Ratty and his family. As the last snake passed where we were hiding we ran out and started biting them. This certainly took them by surprise. As soon as the snakes turned to fight us Ratty and his family came back to give us a hand.

After a while the snakes realised that they were outnumbered and two of them tried to escape. They headed towards the lake. Perhaps they felt that the water was the safest place. As soon as they slithered out of the long grass Oscar and Olive swooped down and with their long claws they grabbed the snakes around their necks and flew off with them. At least they could not bite the owls because they could not move their heads.

When they had gone quite some distance away they dropped them. Then they flew back, grabbed two more and flew off again. When there were only two snakes left and they were just about to pick up Nasty Bob and his mate to take them away as well, Bob said that he wanted to talk to us. So we stopped the attack and listened to what he had to say. He said that he knew they had been very bad but it was the only way that they knew. Also his partner was very upset because the owls had taken all of her family away and she was worried about them. Were they still alive and where were they?

After a long talk we all decided that the fight was over. We had won. Also Olive and Oscar were willing to take the two snakes to where their family were. But we did make them promise to change their ways and also never to come to our part of the forest again.

Not very long afterwards when everything was back to normal we met Max and Mary who told us that they had some new eggs to hatch. Also Derek and Deirdre

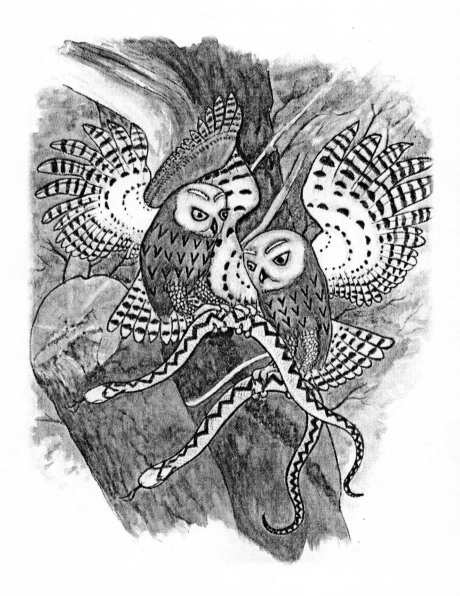

*Oscar and Olive swooped down and with their long claws they grabbed the snakes around their necks and flew off with them.*

said that their chicks were doing well. Ratty Rats family had some new babies on the way and David and Dorothy felt that it was safe to bring their foal to feed by the lake again.

Oscar and Olive fly over the area where the nasty snakes were dropped sometimes, just to let them know that we were still watching them. But I am pleased to say that they have not bothered us since.

Well that's it for today. I hope that you enjoyed my story. Just remember that bullies always lose out in the end.

Bye for now

Sue Kettle.

Mummy Otter.

# CHAPTER FOURTEEN

# THE WOLVES ARE LOOSE

Hello again children. I hope you are well and happy today. Now I would like to tell you a story about a pack of wolves that escaped from their compound and found their way to my part of the forest

When the panthers escaped a short while ago, it took a lot of help from all of our friends to get them caught and taken to a safe place. But there were only two of them. The wolves are not going to be caught as easily. They are even more crafty than the panthers and there are about twenty of them. They have been loose for about three years now and of course they have babies every year. So there will be even more of them now.

The story began one very stormy evening in the New Forest. The wind howled and the rain poured down. There was thunder and lightening that lit up the sky for miles around.

Fortunately for us we had a well built home and of course we love water. We are very strong swimmers, which is very important for us as we catch fish every day for food.

The wolves were kept in a large compound quite a few miles away in another part of the forest. They lived most of the time without interference from the humans who put them there. The large compound was erected to keep the wolves in and to keep all the animals on the outside safe from them. The wolves are pack animals. They hunt in packs and kill their food before eating it

During the night the lightening struck the fence surrounding the compound. Unfortunately a large piece fell down. This left a gap that the wolves soon escaped through.

One family group of about fifteen soon disappeared into the night. By the time the forest rangers spotted the hole and fixed it the wolves were quite a long way from the compound. The Rangers did a check to see just how many had escaped and soon found that Wilf Wolf and his family were missing. They sent out a search party to find them, but the forest is huge and so they had little chance of seeing them again for a long time.

Not long after they escaped, we found out that they had moved quite near to our area and had set up home there.

Oscar Owl who spotted them prowling around near by warned us about their arrival. Also Mike Magpie was keeping his eye on them.

Bertie Boar and his brothers met with Wilf Wolf and several of his family. They did not like each other at all but after a lot of growling and grunting they settled down to talk. So far there had not been any fighting.

The wolves eventually agreed to catch all of their

food outside of our area. But we did not trust them one little bit. They would have to travel quite a way every day to feed. None of us expected them to keep to their side of the agreement.

After a few days as we expected a few rabbits disappeared from the nearby warren. Now we usually loose some rabbits to the humans now and again but not as many as this. Before many more days had passed we had even more bad news. The wolves had killed four young deer and eaten them. They had been ambushed while they were drinking at the lake. They did not stand a chance, but at least the adult deer managed to get away. They must have felt really awful having to run and leave their young to the wolves. But there was nothing that they could do. The wolves would have killed them as well if they had tried to help their young.

We got Oscar and Olive Owls to pass on a message to all the creatures in our area. Mike Magpie helped pass the message around. The idea was for as many animals as possible should go to the lakes to drink. Some of the local birds would keep a look out from in the trees. This would help everyone feel safer.

This was easy for some of the animals such as the wild boar or the New Forest ponies. But not so easy for the rabbits, the ducks, geese, swans and even us because we were less able to protect ourselves from such big violent creatures.

The larger creatures could defend themselves by staying in groups. The wolves were less likely to attack large creatures that stayed together.

Over the next few days the danger became worse. Robbie and myself left home as little as possible. The chances of getting caught grew every day. The wolves were getting very hungry. They were becoming desperate for food. We only went to the lake twice a day to feed and then went straight back to our home and safety. Our children were banned from leaving the home at all as the wolves would soon have them for dinner. We had to fish for ourselves and then catch enough for our children as well. This made a lot of extra work for us but we could not risk the children going out at the moment.

Every day the wolves got hungrier and angrier as they could catch so little food to eat. Eventually they got so hungry that they even attacked the wild boar. They tried to take them by surprise whilst they were eating. As soon as the attack began they were in trouble. Bertie Boar and his family were ready for them. They charged the wolves with such a show of force that they fled into the forest with their tails between their legs. At least the Boar family had shown the wolves that they were not easily beaten.

But hungry wolves are not easily beaten either, as the New Forest ponies were soon to find out.

The same day but a couple of hours later as the ponies were resting after they had eaten a good lunch, the wolves struck hard and fast. The ponies were feeling a bit sleepy and lazy as is normal after dinner. The wolves knew this was the best time to attack. They felt certain that they would soon be having pony for lunch. One pony should be enough to feed the whole family for one whole day.

They spotted one pony with his eyes closed and a bit further away from the main group. Six of the wolves pounced at once. The pony tried to get up and run but

*They spotted one pony with his eyes closed and a bit further away from the main group.*

he had no chance at all. They surrounded him and all attacked at the same time. They soon got him down onto the ground. The rest of the wolves were running between the other ponies frightening them. This worked very well because the other ponies all ran for their lives. They ran as fast as they possibly could to get away from the wolves.

That one poor pony fed the wolves that day. The others had no chance to help him. They did the right thing by running to safety.

Somehow we had to find a way to stop them. We needed to get them out of our area for good. Never to return here for any reason ever.

That night as I lay cuddled up to Robbie and our children, I was thinking what to do when I suddenly remembered something from the past that might be just the way to save us from these awful wolves.

A few years ago we had a forest fire a few miles away from here. This caused a family of bad tempered snakes to come and live in our area. It took a lot of help from the other creatures to get rid of them. But when they did go away, they realised that we had only been protecting our families. We could have had them killed as well as their children, but decided to give them another chance. Also Oscar and Olive helped to carry them safely to another part of the forest where they could start again.

Perhaps now they could help us with our problem. It had to be worth a try. The next morning we spoke to Oscar and Olive and asked them to fly across the forest to where the adders were now living. I sent a message asking them for some help.

A while later Oscar and Olive came back to the lake as we were catching breakfast. At first we thought they were carrying sticks in their claws. But it was two of the adder family. They had come to see if they could help. Oscar suggested carrying them, as it would save a lot of time. After a long talk the adders said that they would love to help us to try to get the wolves to go away for good.

We sent word to all the other creatures that we could reach. Mike Magpie and his family helped as much as they could. Oscar and Olive flew one way while Mike and his family flew the other. They soon had the message passed all around. The other creatures were to meet by the big lake the following morning. We would meet out in the open with lots of lookouts high in the trees. The smaller creatures were to be in the middle of the group with the larger animals surrounding them. The wolves were asked to meet us there just after daylight.

This plan may seem strange at the moment but just wait and see. I think the wolves thought they were going to make a nice meal out of some of us. You see we did not tell them of all our plans. That would have been very silly wouldn't it?

During the night Oscar Owl's family all flew to the adder's home and gave them a lift to the long grass around the lake. They stayed quiet and still and waited for Oscar to give them the signal.

We waited nervously for the wolves to arrive. When they came we could see that they were angry and very hungry. They had not come to talk. They had come to eat. (Us)

The wolves surrounded us and said that we either let

them have at least one of us for breakfast or they would just help themselves.

The Boar family said for everyone to stand still. He knew that the rabbits as well as a lot of the birds just wanted to get as far away as possible. But we all knew that we had to make a stand or we would never be safe again. So no one moved a muscle.

I called to Oscar and he gave the signal to the adders. They all came out of the long grass and bracken and headed for the wolves. There were snakes everywhere. The wolves could not get past them to get away and could not get past Bertie Boar and his family who were backed up by the ponies, to escape. Now it was their turn to be scared. (At last)

Now we had the upper hand. The wolves could not go anywhere without getting hurt.

We could easily have asked the adders to attack and kill the wolves but that is not how we live our lives. So we got the wolves leaders to come and talk to us. We said that as long as they went further into the forest, as far away as possible and promise never to come back again that we would let them go.

They quickly discussed this with their families and decided that they had no choice at all. We had beaten them by sticking together.

The plan was for Bertie Boar and his family to escort them to the edge of our territory and then the Owls would follow them for quite a few miles to make sure they were far enough away from us. They promised that they would never again come into our part of the forest.

So far they have kept their promise. Well that's all for now children. I hope that you enjoyed my little story.

Just remember that by sticking together and helping each other you not just help your friends but yourselves as well.

Bye bye for now.

Sue Kettle.

Mummy Otter.

# CHAPTER FIFTEEN

# THIN ICE

Hello again children. Do you like the lovely sunny days best. Or do you prefer the cold frosty, snowy type of days.

Here in The New Forest the summers are lovely, but the winters are a bit bleak. But at least in the winter we do not get nearly as many humans here. Sometimes humans make us feel very unsafe. They tend to leave litter all over the place and this can be very dangerous to us. Open tin cans and broken glass can cut our feet. But when they are not here we can go about our usual daily routine without being so afraid.

That is in usual winters but not the one am going to tell you about.

A couple of years ago we had a very cold snowy frosty winter. It is a good job that we have thick fur coats to keep us warm. There was a lot of snow everywhere and the lakes were frozen over. This made it very difficult for us to catch fish to eat, so most of the time we went hunting in the rivers.

One day as we were passing the big lake on our way to catch breakfast, when we noticed that a group of humans were camping nearby. We did think this a bit strange for this time of the year. Usually humans only camp here in the better weather. But they are strange creatures aren't they.

We did not worry too much about them being there as we are used to humans being around us. But we would keep a watch on them just in case.

After catching breakfast in the river, the children had a wash and decided to play while Robbie and I had a rest. Just then along came Oscar and Olive owls. They landed quite close to us and asked if we had seen the campers by the big lake. There were two cars with two people in each. They had got out two tents and had several heaters with them. They would certainly need those at night.

A couple of days later when we were on our way to catch breakfast, out of the bracken hopped Ricky and Rita rabbits. They seemed very distressed and both tried to talk at the same time.

"Slow down" I told them. "Just one at a time and I might be able to understand you." I said calmly. Rick eventually managed to tell us that the humans by the big lake were putting animal traps all over the place. In fact Rita almost got caught in one. Fortunately she spotted the wire just in time. We decided to get some help from some of the other animals who lived nearby. Olive and Oscar owls spoke to some of the other birds and decided to keep watch twenty-four hours a day from now on. Then we could see where the traps were being put. This way we could possibly destroy them before any of us got caught. Roger rat and his family volunteered to help us pull the poles out of the ground and bury the traps set for the rabbits. While Benny Badger and his three big sons would use their size and strength to destroy any other traps that were found.

We hoped that if the humans did not have enough food that they would go away. What we could not understand was why they needed to kill us animals to eat. Surely they had enough food with them. They carried some big sacks out of the cars, dug a hole and put the sacks in. Then they filled in the hole again. What was in the sacks if it wasn't food? Why do humans bring so much stuff with them?

We started getting rid of the traps straight away. It was fortunate that no animals or birds had been caught so far.

Robbie and I started pulling the rabbit traps out of the ground and the youngsters carried them to a hole that Benny Badger had dug. Roger Rat and his family were doing the same a little further around the lake. A couple of hours later we were sure that we had either buried or smashed all of the traps. So now it was up to the birds to let us know if the humans put any more out.

It was early next morning that Robbie spoke to Oscar owl to see if the humans had been out during the night. It seems that they had slept well. So no new traps for us to destroy at the moment. Thank goodness for that. I got the children ready and Robbie led the way to the river for our breakfast. Unfortunately it was very misty this morning so we stayed close together. We did not want the children to get lost. Especially with those strange humans around.

After breakfast I made sure the children washed

themselves properly. They tried to get away with a quick lick and then hid in the mist. But I was watching too closely for them to do that.

We were on our way home when we heard the noise. This noise is the worst we can ever hear. It was gunfire. Two shots, probably from a shotgun and quite near to us. I told the children to follow me and to stay very close. Robbie was behind them to make sure they did not get lost in the mist. In no time at all we were home safe and sound, but out of breathe. Robbie said that we should stay as still and quiet as possible until he thought it was safe. They were so scared that they did exactly as they were told. This certainly was a first for them. Bless them.

As there were no more shots heard, after awhile Robbie decided to have a look around. We were not to go out until he came back and told us it was safe to do so. As Robbie crept nearer to the humans he was startled as Cecil Crow suddenly appeared out of the mist. He said that the humans had crept down to the river while the mist was thickest. When Gertie goose flew down to feed, they opened fire on her. She was hit by some of the pellets but managed to fly away to safety. George goose says she should be OK in a few days.

So the humans were still-hunting for food! Why did they not go to the nearest town and buy some? Also what was in those sacks that they buried? Somehow we had to find out. We had a word with Bertie Boar and Benny Badger and came up with a plan. Just a short time later Cecil Crow confirmed that the four men were near their tents sitting around a campfire drinking something hot. They did not seem to have any food with them. We were told that they had put the gun in one of the cars. So we should all be safe when we put our plan into action.

Cecil Crow gave Bertie Boar the signal. This signal was to tell him that Benny Badger was hiding nearby in the bracken. As soon as he got the signal he charged out of the trees towards the four men. He had about fifteen of his family following him. They had crept to within fifty yards of the campfire so it only took them a short time to reach the humans. He made sure that when the four started to run they could not get to the cars. This was to ensure that they could not get to the gun.

Bertie and his family kept on chasing them for some time. He wanted to give us as much time as possible to fulfil our part of the plan. As soon as the men started running, Benny Badger ran to where the humans had buried the sacks and started to dig. In no time at all he reached the first sack with his powerful paws. With one swipe the sack split open and out poured wads of human money. All the packs of paper money were marked with a fifty.

I grabbed a couple of packs with my teeth and so did Robbie. Benny covered the rest of the money again and we all ran off. Benny went home with his family and we went back home to our children. They were waiting quietly but a bit scared. They were so pleased to see us safe and sound. We put the money in the corner and hugged our youngsters for ages.

We went to the river for some lunch and afterwards met up with some of the other creatures to discuss our next move. The children were running everywhere. They had lots of extra energy after staying at home for so long. Thank goodness Bertie boars children were there to play with them. I think they would not have given us any peace at all if Berties youngsters had been too busy to enjoy a game with them.

At the meeting we agreed that the humans were up to no good. They had lots and lots of money, which they buried, but they had no food. Why did they not buy some? Why try to kill us animals to eat? The best suggestion was for us to alert the Forest Rangers about the men. If they should not be there, the Rangers would soon get rid of them. That way we would be safe again.

Robbie and I decided to use the money we got out of the hole to attract the Rangers and get them to follow us to the camp-site where the four men were. First thing next morning we gathered lots of our friends together and finalized our plan.

Robbie and I would take the money to where the Rangers lived. Then somehow we had to get them to follow us. Oscar and Olive Owls said they would help us. Then if the Rangers started to loose us in the bracken or mist then they could help. Also Deirdre Deer followed us. So off we went, after all the other animals and birds had their own special jobs sorted. Everyone seemed to want to help.

When Robbie and I reached the Rangers hut we noticed that Olive and Oscar were already there. So we handed them some of the money, which they held in their beaks. Robbie and I kept the rest in our mouths. Now I asked Deirdre Deer to use her back hooves to bang loudly on the door. "Be careful not to kick it down" joked Robbie. Bang, bang, bang went her hooves. Within seconds the door opened and a very surprised Ranger saw a deer with two owls on her back. Both of these owls had fifty pound notes in their beaks. Also as he looked down he cast his eyes over two otters with lots of fifty pound notes in their mouths. He was certainly more than surprised. He called to someone in the hut. Out came another Ranger. He was carrying a cup of drink in his hands. Well he was until he saw us. Then he promptly dropped it. I do not think he had ever seen anything like it before.

Robbie and I stood on our back legs and danced around and around. Then we ran to the gate. "I think they have got the idea" said Robbie. He almost choked when he spoke because his mouth was still full of money. Deirdre Deer led the way with Robbie and myself close behind. Oscar and Olive flew from tree to tree so they could keep the Rangers in sight. When we were about 1000 metres from the campsite we saw Cecil Crow waiting in the low branches of a walnut tree.

I shouted to him to tell the others creatures to get going with the plan. So off he flew, squawking like mad. Then the forest all around the campsite seemed to come alive. There were creatures of all sorts running and flying towards the two tents. The four men were sitting around a campfire, but not for long. When all of our friends started running and flying towards them, shouting, squealing and squawking and making any noise possible to frighten them. The men started running along the bank of the lake but Roger Rat had already run ahead of them, with at least eighty of his family.

When the men saw them running towards them they turned and headed the other way. Only to find a mass of swans, geese, ducks and other birds all flapping madly toward them. Followed by twenty angry badgers.

Now they were trapped. Rats from the left, thirty wild boar from the front, birds from the right backed up by the badgers.

The Rangers were certain that the animals would kill the men. But we only wanted them to be captured. Of course the four men did not know this did they.

The only place to escape was across the ice on the lake. So the men turned and ran onto the ice. This was a very big mistake on their part. The ice was quite thick near the bank but not so a few yards out. As expected the ice gave way and all four of them ended up to their chests in very, very cold water.

As soon as the Rangers got to the edge of the lake they helped the four men struggle onto the bank. Freezing cold, soaking wet and shivering. One of the Rangers must have called for help because just then along came two police cars with lots of help. It was only then that we noticed Benny Badger digging furiously where the sacks were buried. The Rangers handed the four sorry figures over to the police and then went to where Benny Badger was digging.

Benny stood back when he had dug down to the sacks. One of the Rangers reached into hole and pulled out one of the sacks. He looked inside, saw all that money and called the police officers over.

Just then another police officer opened the boot of one of the cars and pulled out the shotgun. Of course most of the animals and birds that had been watching from close bye knew how dangerous to us this gun could be. One of the Rangers must have seen the horror in our faces, because he shouted to the officer to the relief of us all. Then the four men were taken away with the cars and of course the money.

We thanked all of our friends for their help and went home knowing that we should be a lot safer from now on. The next day as we were taking the children to the river to feed, we noticed eight Forest Rangers by the lake. They were smashing lots of ice from all around the edge. This meant that we had time to dive in and feed well before it froze over again. There was a lot more fish in the lake than in the river, so we certainly did not miss out on the chance for a big breakfast.

Also to our surprise, they came back every day until the thaw came. The other creatures have told me that they have found extra food left out for them every day as well. We assume the Rangers are saying thanks for our help. Isn't that nice?

Well that's all for now children. Just remember that guns can be dangerous. So can greed.

Bye for now, until the next time.

Sue Kettle.

Mummy Otter.

Printed in the United Kingdom
by Lightning Source UK Ltd.
9853100001B/37